MISADVENTURES WITH THE DUKE

Forever Yours Series

STACY REID

MISADVENTURES WITH THE DUKE is a work of fiction. While reference might be made to actual historical events or existing locations, the names, characters, places, and incidents are either the product of the author's imagination or are used fictitiously, and any resemblance to actual persons, living or dead, business establishments, events, or locales are entirely coincidental.

All rights reserved. No part of this book may be reproduced in any form by any electronic or mechanical means—except in the case of brief quotations embodied in critical articles or reviews—without written permission.

First Edition January 2019

Edited by AuthorsDesigns
Copy-edited by Gina Fiserova
Cover design and formatting by AuthorsDesigns
Stock art from Period Images
Copyright © 2019 by Stacy Reid

Dusean, always and forever.

PRAISE FOR NOVELS OF
STACY REID

"**Duchess by Day, Mistress by Night** is a sensual romance with explosive chemistry between this hero and heroine!"—*Fresh Fiction Review*

"From the first page, Stacy Reid will captivate you! Smart, sensual, and stunning, you will not want to miss **Duchess by Day, Mistress by Night**!"—*USA Today bestselling author Christi Caldwell*

"I would recommend **The Duke's Shotgun Wedding** to anyone who enjoys passionate, fast-paced historical romance."—*Night Owl Reviews*

"**Accidentally Compromising the Duke**—Ms. Reid's story of loss, love, laughter and healing is all that I look for when reading romance and deserving of a 5-star review."—*Isha C., Hopeless Romantic*

PRAISE FOR NOVELS OF STACY REID

"**Wicked in His Arms**—Once again Stacy Reid has left me spellbound by her beautifully spun story of romance between two wildly different people."—*Meghan L., LadywithaQuill.com*

"**Wicked in His Arms**—I truly adored this story and while it's very hard to quantify, this book has the hallmarks of the great historical romance novels I have read!"—*KiltsandSwords.com*

"One for the ladies...**Sins of a Duke** is nothing short of a romance lover's blessing!"—*WTF Are You Reading*

"**THE ROYAL CONQUEST** is raw, gritty and powerful, and yet, quite unexpectedly, it is also charming and endearing."—*The Romance Reviews*

OTHER BOOKS BY STACY

Sinful Wallflowers series
My Darling Duke

Forever Yours series
The Marquess and I
The Duke and I
The Viscount and I
Misadventures with the Duke
When the Earl was Wicked
A Prince of my Own
Sophia and the Duke
The Sins of Viscount Worsley

The Kincaids
Taming Elijah
Tempting Bethany
Lawless: Noah Kincaid

Rebellious Desires series
Duchess by Day, Mistress by Night
The Earl in my Bed

Wedded by Scandal Series
Accidentally Compromising the Duke
Wicked in His Arms
How to Marry a Marquess

Scandalous House of Calydon Series
The Duke's Shotgun Wedding
The Irresistible Miss Peppiwell
Sins of a Duke
The Royal Conquest

The Amagarians
Eternal Darkness
Eternal Flames
Eternal Damnation
Eternal Phoenyx

Single Titles
Letters to Emily
Wicked Deeds on a Winter Night
The Scandalous Diary of Lily Layton

CHAPTER 1

London, 1839

The *haut monde* of London no longer whispered whenever Miss Phillipa Beatrice Cavanaugh— Pippa to friends and family— made one of her rare appearances in society. Tonight, at Lady Peregrine's midnight ball, the hushed words repeating her family's history no longer rode the air, cutting against her skin, and burrowing into her heart. Their eyes however still gleamed with speculation, judgment, and perhaps pity. As it stood only a few lords and ladies of society made overtures to welcome Pippa and her mamma, Lady Lavinia Cavanaugh, within their elevated circles despite her being the daughter of a Baron, Lord Rupert Cavanaugh.

Correction...the daughter of a disgraceful runaway Baron.

Pippa's scandal was not the typical one that

haunted most society families—the reckless racing, gambling debts, a deliberate compromising, or an elopement to Gretna Green. Pippa, at only two and twenty, suffered from a tarnished reputation these last several years because of a selfish decision her father had made. The consequences had also reduced Pippa and her mother to genteel poverty. Her father's modest estate in Hertfordshire hung in limbo and disrepair, for he'd abandoned them to live with the woman he loved in America. He had written to Pippa over the years, informing her of the two children he had with his wealthy American mistress, and while Pippa's mother bitterly called them her husband's *little bastards*, a part of Pippa yearned to know her siblings.

Still, the dreadful scandal resulting from her father's decision followed them like the foulest of airs. It was as if his inconsistency and dishonor would one day show in her blood. In the five years since her father left them, the pain and disgrace of it all had seen mamma insisting they seclude themselves in the heart of the country, ignoring all invitations to town, and the indulgence of the season. Despite their steward's best effort to keep the estate solvent, they'd been informed the coffers were nigh on empty.

When her mother had wearily informed her it was time to marry, Pippa hadn't rebelled, wanting to escape the shame and pain of her papa's decision, and forge another path for herself. Perhaps there would be a new adventure within marriage, a happier life, a fresh beginning. Anything would undoubtedly be better than the tedium of country life, where she took long walks, attended church, and balls at the local assembly. The only bright spot was the romantic comedy she wrote, solely based on the life of the people in her idyllic village—Crandleforth.

In truth, the people of Crandleforth almost made their village feel like home. There, no one blamed them for her father's dishonor, and they were treated as faithful friends, family even. But Pippa still wanted to leave. Surely there was more to life than the everyday humdrum of Crandleforth and its citizens, even the pleasant ones.

Quite irritated with herself for remembering the sly, cruel murmurs that had rabidly whispered of her family's misfortune, Pippa pinned a small smile on her lips and tapped her feet ever so slightly to the dazzling and invigorating music leaping to life from the orchestras' bow. Tonight should be about the future, not wallowing in the past.

She'd been in town a week now, and the glitter and dazzle of the season had been beyond incredible. Tonight's ball was hosted in a grand ballroom at the base of a wide gold railed staircase, which allowed the viewing of all the guests entering, who were dressed in the height of fashion displaying their wealth with their elegant and elaborate jeweled accessories. Several golden chandeliers descended from the ceiling covered in a mural depicting the sky with a multitude of hues aesthetically blended together.

Footmen moved through the crush bearing endless refreshments, there was laughter, chittering, and dancing. Merriment all about. This was indeed a welcomed change from the dull, yet peaceful, Crandleforth.

"Oh Pippa, I am distressed no one has asked you to dance," a hushed voice whispered to her left. "You are one of the prettiest girls here tonight! I've had six dances, and my feet are begging for relief, and you've had no requests. Why I truly cannot credit."

Lady Miranda, a dear childhood friend, stepped to her side and looped her hand through Pippa's. Her friend did not mean it unkindly, it was a simple observation. And Pippa expected Miranda's dance card to always be filled. She was slender and graceful with her golden hair piled high in a riot of fashionable curls, quite beautiful, and much coveted by the young bucks. She'd already received three offers this season. All had been rejected for the family had higher hopes for their daughter.

"I do not mind. I see no one worth the honor." And Pippa was anticipating a very particular gentleman making a sort of declaration tonight. That was why she had been so keen on attending, despite her dismal reception at another ball three days ago, and a musicale only yesterday.

Vibrant green eyes peered down at Pippa's much shorter frame.

"Oh, I do feel so wretched, Pippa, to be having so much fun when you are only observing."

"I take joy in watching the dances, you know I have two left feet. I am sure to stomp on toes," she teased.

Miranda rolled her eyes in an unladylike fashion, which if her mother the Countess Leighton had seen, would have incited vapors and sharp corrections. It was a wonder the countess who expected perfection from her daughter, allowed her such friendship with the imperfect Pippa. Though she knew it was because of the more than decade-long friendship between the countess and her mother. Several summers as a child, Pippa had traveled to the countess's country home in Lincolnshire, and it was there the treasured friendship had grown with Miranda. Pippa was happy the countess hadn't turned away from them when the scandal had broke. She had remained mamma's true and dearest friend.

Miranda squeezed her arm. "There is a buzz about the room that the Duke of Carlyle would be in attendance tonight, and that is quite a coup for Lady Peregrine. But I've yet to see him, and oh I do so want to!"

"Miranda do behave! And what shall you do if you see the duke?"

Pippa's friend smiled mischievously, tucking a ringlet of hair behind her ear. "Why flirt shamelessly with him, of course. I've met him previously, and I declare we would be a perfect fit! He is so dashing and handsome! Mamma would be quite pleased with me if I snagged his attention. Imagine me, a duchess! How lovely it would be."

Pippa had a particular weakness for scandal sheets, and those pages spent an inordinate amount of time on the wickedly handsome but very boring Christopher Worth, the Duke of Carlyle. A man Miranda seemed determined to set her cap at, and the only thing that seemed to recommend him to the position was his title.

Pippa wondered if she should caution her friend to be circumspect in her admiration for a man the scandal sheet lamented might never marry. It seemed he could not find a lady as tedious, exacting, and proper as himself. The tattle sheets had never reported anything remotely scandalous on the man, yet they seemed compelled to mention his very private activities weekly. Why, only last week they spoke of his visit to a circulating library. Pippa was still uncertain as to why that was newsworthy, though she guiltily admitted she had devoured the article.

Miranda craned her elegant neck, peering at someone in the crowded ballroom. "I see Lady Shelly. I must confer with her. Would you like to accompany me?"

"I dare not," Pippa said. "I am a trifle overheated and may slip onto the terrace."

Miranda nodded and made her way through the crowd, heading toward the bobbing purple turban by the refreshment table. With a sigh, Pippa glanced around, searching for the particular gentleman she had attended solely for tonight—Mr. Nigel James Williamsfield. Tonight all would be well, and everyone would see that she and her mother had recovered quite nicely from *the disaster*—the name the polite world, the newspapers, and scandal sheets had dubbed the pain that had torn through their family with such terrible, rending teeth.

Tonight, Nigel would declare for her in front of the polite world, and he would do this by just asking for Pippa's hand in a dance. How utterly simple but so complicated. Across the crowded ballroom, she met the eyes of her mother who winked and lifted her chin toward the upper levels. Pippa gasped when she spied him descending the wide staircase to the ball floor, and she had to prevent herself from pushing through the crowd to go to him. He had taken so long to reach the ball she'd doubted he would attend. Pippa laughed softly and suppressed the urge to twirl with the dizzying excitement rushing through her veins.

It was not that she sought the approval of the *ton*, but there was a deep part of her heart that wished for everyone to see that she was indeed acceptable. That the scandal did not mean that she was tainted, unlovable, or unmarriable as they had whispered for months. No gentleman required dances of her, asked her to stroll in the park or to accompany them on carriage rides. No bouquets of roses and lilies filled the hallways and parlors for her the morning after a ball. Now, a single dance with Nigel would show everyone that she was indeed marriageable and acceptable to his esteemed family despite the past scandal.

She had met him a few months past, and he had become her dearest friend for several weeks while they had taken long walks in the countryside in Crandleforth. How amiable and accepting he had been, and unflinching in his courtship when he had learned of her impoverished circumstances, and less than ideal reputation.

Her mother who had despaired of her ever securing a match had started to hope. And if Pippa were to be honest, she hadn't believed marriage a possibility for her though she had hungered for a family of her own. A husband to love, and children with whom she could share the many stories she had crafted over the years for her entertainment.

Her gaze collided with Nigel, and she couldn't help smiling widely. It had been over four weeks since they had last communicated, and Pippa had despaired that she should ever travel to London and had told him so in a letter. He'd replied, professing his love and how much he would miss her, and had lamented how droll the balls were without her presence. How thrilled he would be to see that she had managed to travel to town. They'd let their townhouse in Mayfair for the last three years to a merchant family to Mamma's embarrassment. Mamma had prevailed upon her dear friend Lady Leighton, and they currently stayed with the countess at her townhouse in Russell Square.

Her smile faltered when Nigel stared through her before glancing away. An awful sensation lodged itself in the vicinity of her heart. Surely, she was mistaken as to think he would ignore her presence. Though they hadn't spoken about it, Pippa had not been led to believe he would ignore her in a public setting.

Lifting her chin, she determined to be patient and not hasten to a conclusion. However, several minutes passed, and that heavy sensation pressing against her chest had spread to encompass her entire body. Her mother appeared stricken as Nigel passed her without acknowledging her even once. He made the rounds, and it was easy to see he was quite a popular gentleman.

It seemed so inconceivable she had been mistaken in his affection and attention. He had declared himself to her several times, and he had made it known to her mother he intended to court her. In fact, her mamma had been despondent in spirits for the last several months, and it had been Nigel's presence in their lives which had seen her rallying.

Pippa plucked a glass of champagne from a passing footman and took several indelicate sips. Oh! Relief swept through her when she espied him coming her way with his mother, Viscountess Perth. Feeling sorry she had ever doubted him, Pippa lifted her gaze to his and awaited his approach without displaying they had knowledge of each other. A soft gasp escaped her when he passed by so closely, she could have brushed the lapel of his dark evening jacket. He stopped only a few paces from her, bowed to the elegantly charming Miss Elinor Darwhimple, and requested her hand in a dance.

Pippa wanted to die from the humiliation and pain crawling through her but perversely refused to run away. Several minutes passed while she stood on the sidelines, watching her mother attempting the same feat—trying to be brave amidst a sea of confusion and dashed hopes. Pippa startled when a footman approached her and discreetly slipped her a note.

She strolled toward a column and peeked at the note.

Meet me in the conservatory. And there it was, the drawing of a rose as Nigel's signature, same as in all the letters he had ever sent her. Fury pounded through her veins, the sudden rush burning away all pain and shame she had felt. *How dare he!*

She scanned the room to see him watching her. With deliberate slowness, she tore the note into small pieces. He glanced away, bowing to the three ladies who approached him. Crumpling the little bits of papers in her hand, hating that her throat burned with unshed tears, she pushed through the crowd needing to escape for a breath of fresh air. Yet she did not hasten to the wide-open terraced doors leading out into the gardens. Instead, she made her way from the ballroom and down the surprisingly empty hallway. Pippa and Miranda had accompanied the countess on a call to Lady Peregrine for tea a couple of weeks ago, so Pippa tried to recall which door had led to the library.

Instinctively she knew being surrounded by books, she would be able to breathe, and perhaps the tight knot constricting her heart up to her throat would ease. Upon reaching the large oak door, polite habit insisted she knock, though it was quite unlikely anyone else would be in the library. When no voice called out, she eased the door open and slipped inside. The large room was awash with pale moonlight which painted half of the room in muted shades of silver and moonbeams. The embers in the large fireplace barely flickered. She strolled over to the wide-open windows, uncaring of the slight chill in the air.

The door opened, and she whirled around. She discerned the features of Nigel.

The shock had her stiffening.

"Pippa, my darling, I—"

"You followed me?"

He faltered at her sharp question. "I had to, my sweet, when I saw you tore up my note, I had to."

"You will refer to me as Miss Cavanaugh, sir, nor will you come closer," she snapped furiously when he made to advance further into the barely lit room.

He paused, and they stared at each other in tense silence. She so very badly wanted to demand he leave or slip through the windows herself to escape this confrontation. Pippa feared what his actions tonight meant, the ruination of all the dreams and hope which had been bubbling in her heart these several weeks. But she was not a coward, and she would not start acting like one now. The truth must be had, even if the pain of it broke her heart. "Why did you not seek an introduction or ask me for a dance? You pretended not to know me, as if we had no attachment."

She wasn't sure if he flinched or if it was a trick of the light.

"Pippa—"

"Miss Cavanaugh," she said, hating how husky with pain her voice sounded.

"I...I am to be married," he finally said.

She stared uncomprehendingly for several moments before accepting he meant to someone else. That could indeed be his only meaning, but she had to ask, "To someone else?"

He raked his fingers through his light brown hair, creating a mess of what had been perfectly styled. "Yes. To Elinor Darwhimple."

The shock that tore through Pippa rendered her to a marble. "It has been announced?"

"Not as yet. But we have an understanding, and the negotiations between our families are completed. The announcement will be sent to the newspapers tomorrow."

She stared at him in muted hurt and disappointment, a desperate feeling of unreality creeping through her. Finally, her lips parted, and she said, "You said you wanted to marry *me*...you even told my mother..." she swayed, the ruined dreams settling on her shoulders like a boulder. "You said you loved me and wanted to marry me."

He hurried forward to take her gloved hand in his. "And when I declared myself and asked for a kiss, you said you did not love me as yet," he reminded her with sickening earnestness as if that would excuse his offensive conduct. "You did not return my sentiments in the way I had hoped, my darling. Surely you see that I was confused by your lack of ardor and encouragement."

No...she hadn't loved him as yet, not in the way the poets described it, in the manner her mother still yearned for her father. But Pippa had liked and enjoyed all Nigel's amiable qualities, had believed in his declared affections, and had believed love...the most passionate sort would inevitably follow. She was suddenly grateful that their skin made no contact and she hadn't kissed him when he'd asked. He did not deserve such a privilege.

He had been so friendly and obliging, always seeking her company. Standing up to dance with her at the balls held at the town's assembly hall. The citizens of Crandleforth had smelled a union on the air and had even started offering congratulations long before it had occurred to Pippa an attachment was forming. Nigel had no intention of declaring for her.

He had merely been amusing himself with a flirtation. Perhaps even a seduction. The *blackguard*.

The sweet, amiable way they had bantered, the laughter, the dancing, and the curricle rides had meant nothing to him. "Every word from you was a lie," she whispered. "I was honest with you, but you were only deceptive." And she had not seen through it! In the same manner, she had never seen that her father no longer loved her and mamma, and his heart had been wholly engaged elsewhere. How could she still be so naïve?

"Please do not doubt my sincerity or affections for you. I promise nothing will change, and I will still provide for you with a townhouse and a carriage with an allowance. I do not want to lose you, and you shan't lose me my sweet," he continued earnestly. "I vow it!"

Pippa felt faint. "You'll provide me with...a carriage and an allowance...." Her voice ended, and she stared at him, distress beating through her veins. She might have spent the last few years in the country, but she had enough experience of how cruel the world could be to know he referred to offering her *carte blanche*. A mistress. "You think to establish me as your soiled dove?"

"Pippa, my darling—"

She pulled her hands from his. "You are a vile, disgusting pig! And I do feel as if I've insulted all the swine in the world by comparing a man such as yourself to them."

This close she could see the flattening of his lips and the darkening of his brown eyes. A flush, evident in the meager moonlight, reddened his jawline. "Pippa—"

Her disgust threatened to choke her. "You will leave my presence immediately, or I will scream. I am certain your soon-to-be fiancée and mother will not appreciate you being discovered in a compromising situation with the likes of me."

A tic appeared in his jaw, and then he turned about and left the room. She hurried toward the door and closed it with a *snick*. A few minutes alone was required with no interruption. Her composure had to be gathered, the tears trembling on her lids suppressed before she braved the outside, and before she faced her mamma. How would she take the news?

Moving away from the door toward the window, Pippa faltered in the center of the library. A choked sob escaped her lips. How foolishly hopeful she had been. She stood there, hating the fact tears coursed down her cheeks. She pressed trembling fingers to her lips, drawing forth on the anger, preferring it to the stabbing pain in her heart. "The insufferable *pig*! That snake...blackguard...baboon!"

A low voice drawled from the darkened corner to her left, "Come now, I am sure you can do better than that."

Pippa screamed.

CHAPTER 2

Her heart in her throat, and a hand covering her mouth, Pippa whirled toward the darkened corner. She flushed in embarrassment and gripped the folds of her gown. Someone had heard her crude and unladylike utterances. And worst, he'd witnessed her shameful and private exchange with Nigel, a scandal even worst than before loomed. She and mamma would never recover.

"A bloody idiotic bacon-brained ass, a blackguard of the highest order, a dishonorable bounder. A pig's arse, a maggot, a scalawag, a pompous lobcock," the voice continued, shocking her silly. "Be free with your curses, I will not tell a soul."

A horrified sound slipped from her and mortification crawled through her at his very vulgar tongue. This man was unpardonable. She briefly glanced back at the door she had just closed, wondering if she attempted to flee if she would make it before the man behind the voice reacted.

"Have I rendered you silent?" he asked with rough amusement.

Pippa honestly had no words.

"How odd, a woman of your...fire seemed to be made of sterner stuff."

Now the tone was mockingly bemused.

Peering in his darkened corner, she lifted her chin. "Who are you, sir?" And how dare he witness such a private moment and not reveal himself. Not the mark of a gentleman at all.

"Ah...are we affecting introductions then?"

She choked, but managed to say, after a brief struggle, "No." Suddenly she did not care to know the identity of the man in the shadows. She inched back toward the door.

The clink of glasses sounded, arresting her movements. Pippa could not say why she stood there or what she waited for. She jerked when the gas lamp switched on, bathing the library in a soft, intimate glow. The man was revealed, and her breath audibly hitched to her great mortification.

He was unquestionably handsome with his sensual mouth, prominent cheekbones, and thick raven-black hair. He was a stranger to her, and apparently a wealthy man of fashion—garbed in black trousers and jacket, with a golden waistcoat, and expertly tied cravat. His raven hair was impeccably styled, curling softly at his nape.

Had she ever seen a gentleman so exquisitely dressed, commanding, and terribly attractive? His lips curved at her unabashed and very impolite regard. The stranger studied her a moment longer, then slowly stood up, straightening to an impressive height of well over six feet. The stranger was tall with broad shoulders, a narrow waist, lean hips, and long legs. He was put together too fine, he really was.

She was painfully aware of him taking several slow, measured steps closer. The sharp lines of his jaw were clean-shaven, revealing every arrogant line of his handsome features. His eyes, which were deep-set, and a striking silver held an expression of faint surprise as he stared at her.

"Hello," he said mildly.

Her heart tripped, and wings of indecision took flight in her stomach. Caution urged her to flee with haste. Pippa had never known such awareness of another gentleman, not even the cad who had just broken her hopes. To escape now, she might encounter a wagging tongue who would speculate on her tear-stained face and evidently wounded eyes. But regardless, if she possessed any wisp of rationality, she would depart immediately.

He held out one of his hands, and she lowered her eyes. He held a glass filled with amber liquid. She snapped her gaze back to his.

"I might scream," she said huskily.

"I am persuaded I may rely on your good sense not to do so. I believe you might need fortification," he said softly, and she blinked at the compassion and lack of judgment in his tone.

She stared, feeling stupefied.

He arched a brow and lifted one of the glass. "I won't tell if you won't."

"It is unladylike to drink," she replied, unsure of his intention, and far more alarmed as to why she was not running. No satisfactory answer presented itself, and her feet remained rooted as if they had a will of their own.

He smiled—a wicked, dangerous smile that made her nerves leap.

"It is also unladylike to curse, and I thought you did rather well for an evident fledging. I was impressed."

Her eyes widened at his gall, and she hated to admit there was a strange but very becoming warmth unfurling somewhere low in her stomach.

He was smiling at her, and, try as she would, she was incapable of resisting the impulse to return that small bit of shared intimacy. How complicated could a smile be? For it hinted at shared amusement and could be an invitation to friendship, a liking, or even more. She was addled. There was no question about it.

He moved a bit closer, and she retreated. He held up the glasses in his hand as if to indicate surrender. "I swear on my honor you have nothing to fear from me, Miss—?"

Pippa snorted as if she would own to her identity.

She was not *that* addled. "No names." A sense of preservation urged her to be anonymous, and she followed it blindly.

"No names," he murmured. "I would urge you to take a steadying drink, compose yourself and then face the sharks. They are ruthless when they smell blood...your eyes are wide and wounded, the pain in them urges me to find that bounder and plant a facer on him. It is evident you are bleeding." He paused significantly. Provoking amusement lit in his eyes—very fine eyes that glowed with intelligence and wickedness. Then he said, "And quite ugly with those tear blotches and red nose."

Pippa gasped, her hand flying to her cheeks, feeling the wet trails and the puffiness under her eyes. Then she scowled. She'd never been a pretty crier, but, "You, sir, are no gentleman!"

He scowled. "Not a gentleman! You dismay me. Was it the ugly comment? Pray tell me what it may be!"

Pippa laughed, the sound so surprised her she gasped.

Now his lips tipped in a charming smile. "Ah... mission partially accomplished. Laughter is its own balm and your smile...I daresay, is even more beautiful," he said quietly.

Who was he? Perversely, she did not want to ask after denying the need for introductions. "I thank you for your kindness, sir, but I must leave." The temptation to stay here with this stranger beat at her, but she couldn't be so reckless and foolish. Quickly before she could change her mind, she hurried over, took the glass from his hand, tipped it to her lips and consumed it in a long swallow.

Pippa wheezed as the fiery flavors exploded on her tongue and slid down her throat. Then she coughed and spluttered. Her mortification was complete, and she could now die. "What is this poison?" she cried in comical dismay, stumbling back, and clutching her chest in mock horror, relying on humor as a shield.

A full-blown smile curved his lips, and she forgot to breathe. "You are far too handsome, sir." Shocked by her own lapse from propriety, she could only stare.

His eyes widened before they were hooded. Then he tipped his glass to his lips and swallowed his drink in a smooth slide. "It's whisky. A most potent balm for the wounded soul."

A story lies behind those dark throbbing words, and she considered him carefully. Who was he truly? "And your soul is wounded?"

The slightest stiffening of his shoulders. "Not anymore."

Suddenly she wished it was proper just to have a conversation of mutually injured hearts. "I'm glad for it. In my experience, they never close you know. There's always a little opening, and the slightest thing can rip it open painfully."

He studied her appraisingly. "Tell me your name,"

he said unexpectedly, his tone imbued with such authority she almost obeyed.

She frowned over this for moment or two, before saying decidedly, "No."

He smiled appreciatively. "I like your bluntness."

Pippa slowly backed up at the wickedness which suddenly glinted in his eyes. She sensed it in the slow, intimate gaze from the tip of her coiffed head, over the icy blue gown she wore, the white half gloves, and the silver dancing slippers. She felt his stare...as if he touched her, as impossible as it seemed. Every womanly instinct for self-preservation surged to life, and her heart tripled in its rhythm. Yet he did not make a move toward her, simply waited.

"I should...no...I *must* leave...now."

An oddly anticipatory silence blanketed the library. An awareness bloomed that he was a man, she was a woman, and wicked deeds happened behind a closed door. The knowledge settled between them, heavy and thick.

An indecipherable emotion passed over his face. "I would hate to mortify your sensibilities any further. Go," he murmured. "Now."

And Pippa turned and fled as if the devil had come knocking and she had considered answering.

⁂

THE SHAPE OF THAT LUSH, very rounded, and *delightful* backside disappearing through the doors would be forever interred in his thoughts. The unknown lady's curves were *lovely*, her eyes the finest he'd ever seen, even when dark with such pain. He indeed had no notion if she was pretty, not with her red nose, cheeks, and swollen eyes. He chuckled mirthlessly. How close he had come to making an idiotic mistake. Christopher Edmund Worth, the Duke of Carlyle closed his eyes and cursed under his breath. He'd thought about kissing the dark-haired stranger with her light gray eyes and pouting lips. She must have seen the loss of control in his eyes or felt his weakness as he had argued with himself against taking her into his arms and kissing her senseless. Otherwise, she might not have fled.

A man was as good as his reputation. As good as the legacy of his family's status, and he had a very old and exacting lineage to live up to, for his family's sake. No public scandal and scrutiny had ever surrounded the Worth family. Well, none that he could recall, not even something as simple, yet so dangerous, as a kiss between two strangers.

A kiss with a stranger at a ball could lead to a compromising situation, an affair, trouble, and *scandal*. And for the last several years he had ensured not a blemish cast itself on his family's legacy because of his actions. The one instance he had not been careful enough his father had almost died. Christopher had never wantonly dishonored or abused the privilege of his rank. But he had fancied himself in love at the age of twenty with an older gypsy girl, Theodosia whom he met on his travels abroad.

She had been his lover for several weeks, and he had enjoyed her witty company and her sensual, adventurous spirit. With her, he had been able to explore the wicked leanings in his heart to be free with his sexual desires. Yearnings which had once confused his young mind had flowered under her passionate tutelage. She had fallen with child, and he had wanted to marry her, to give their child his name and respectability. Theodosia had laughingly refused to marry him, saying she would be free.

Christopher still remembered the shock of his father clutching at his chest and collapsing to the ground. And all he had done was inform his family he would not deny his child upon birth, and he would acknowledge and care for his child. His mother had screamed that it was his wicked, unprincipled ways which caused his father's collapse.

Christ. The very memory of it knotted his stomach. His father had lived and had gone on to his rewards several years' later by retiring to bed and not waking the following morning. His only complaint had been a stomach ailment for a few weeks, and his death had been an unexpected shock. Still, the old duke had had a smile on his lips, and to Christopher's mind, his father had died happy. Not a thing many could wish for. Theodosia had died in childbirth, along with his stillborn daughter. His family had never said it, but how relieved they'd been with that outcome was evident.

He refilled his glass with whisky, taking a healthy swallow.

Since then, as the head of the family, he had been more careful, respecting his family's desire to uphold their pristine reputation. The few lovers he'd had over the years were all discreet, and society had no knowledge of their identity. To the world, he was proper and just, like the many illustrious men of his line, and he had worked to keep it that way.

His family was intolerably unforgiving of anyone who did not fit their idea of proper behavior. It was uncouth and vulgar not to be able to manage one's emotions and passions that could lead to scandal. The men in his family did not indulge in excessive drinking, carriage racing, gambling, public brawls, or private ones for that matter. A willful, hedonistic lifestyle indicated a weakness of character that was abhorrent to his straight-laced family. Weak-blooded fools his grandmother, who was Catholic but kept to the Church of England's rules, had always said scathingly.

And he did see the honor of not being controlled by vices, but he did not believe in abstinence from pleasure. Nor did he allow society and his family to dictate those he should trust and befriend.

And this slip of a girl...no, a woman, with all her bountiful curves and beautiful eyes had tempted him with curse words, a very splotchy skin, and eyes swollen from tears. She was truly an ugly crier. Christopher chuckled. He had lost his damn senses. Emptying the last of the drink, he made his way from the library, down the elegantly appointed hallway before coming upon a wide-open door leading to a large ballroom.

Every single woman in the room had become aware of him the moment he arrived. And while other gentlemen would preen at the attention, their unabashed admiration irritated Christopher. It wasn't his character that turned their heads or made the ladies eager for his company. Only his title and income seemed to be of concern.

The noise and the different scents crashed against his senses. Ladies and gentlemen twirled across the ballroom, glittering in their fineries, many stood on the sidelines laughing and chatting behind their fans. Footmen slipped with impressive dexterity through the crush, serving glasses of champagne. A few young debutantes sent him coy, flirtatious glances, and the older girls and ladies were quite bolder in their regard and expectations. It irritated him that not one of them gave a donkey's arse about what he liked or wanted from life. They merely saw the blasted title and his worth. In truth, the lady in the library just now had been the first in years to stare at him without avarice or manipulation.

His older sister by a year, the charming Selina, Lady Andrews, a marchioness in her own right, a fashion icon for young ladies of the *ton*, hurried over to him and looped her hands within his. Clad in a layered golden gown which clung to her slender frame, her black hair caught in a high pile atop her head styled and threaded with pearls, she appeared quite beautiful and radiant. Though he suspected her glow of happiness should be credited to her recent announcement, for she and her marquis expected their first child seven months from now.

"Christopher darling, you had promised to dance with Miss Charlotte Hufford. She is *perfect* for you," Selina gushed, silver-gray eyes very much like his twinkling merrily. "At least two of the set of waltzes for tonight have already gone. Charlotte was so crushed not to have stood up with you."

"I'm sure she'll recover," he said dryly. If he recalled correctly, Miss Hufford had been the lady to drop her lace handkerchief at his feet earlier in the receiving line. He'd obliged, to her delight, and had then been introduced.

Somehow his family thought Miss Hufford was the ideal woman to be his duchess. How they could fathom he would wish to marry an eighteen-year-old girl in her first season was beyond him. And they would not be deterred in their thoughts or ambitions for him. His two sisters—Amelia and Selina—were happily married to men of rank and fortune, and they would not be content until he was similarly situated it seems. It was perhaps time to stop being indulgent of their matchmaking theatrics. It was becoming tedious as his marriage appeared to be the only topic of exciting conversation whenever they met.

"I'm not interested in dancing with Miss Hufford."

His sister shot him a surprised glance. "At least it sounds like you might be interested in dancing. You haven't stood up with anyone I've urged you to for the last three balls! Is there someone you are interested in and not saying to Amelia or me?" she asked archly, following his gaze, though discreetly done, to the lady in blue.

His sister's arm dug into his, and she audibly gasped. "*That* is Miss Pippa Cavanaugh. How did she secure an invitation I wonder? Her father is Baron Cavanaugh," she whispered, quite aghast. "Surely you recall the disaster?"

In other words, Miss Pippa Cavanaugh was a scandal and disgrace, the opposite to everything his family stood for. Christopher still remembered the scandal which had exploded around the Cavanaughs some five or six years ago. Society had been ruthless and happy in pronouncing judgment.

"How do you know her?" his sister asked, her dulcet tone rich with disapproval.

"I do not," he said blandly. Was this why she had sounded so devastated when that bounder had revealed himself to be a cad? Had she rested her hopes on marrying him?

He tried to wrest his gaze away and could not. The icy blue short-sleeved gown was worn low on her shoulders, the narrow skirt hugging her curvaceous frame to its best advantage. Her raven-black hair was styled in a simple chignon with a few artful curls kissing her rosy cheeks, and unlike the other ladies, she was without diamonds, pearls, and rubies. Miss Cavanaugh might not be dressed in the first stare of fashion as all the other ingénues present, but she was charming in her appearance, and to his mind quite lovely.

"Christopher you are staring," Selina gasped, squeezing his arm. "Good gracious! Do you like her?"

Her tone implied it would be better to say he wished to kiss a two-headed snake. He'd always been frank with his sisters, but now he felt oddly protective of Miss Cavanaugh's reputation. The image of her injured eyes created an ache in the proximity of his heart. "I have not been introduced to the lady," he returned mildly.

"Miss Cavanaugh is not the sort a man of your rank, breeding, and propriety would extend the smallest encouragement, my dear brother. She is neither handsome nor fashionable, and her connections are deplorable!"

"Not handsome, Selina? I've never known you to be petty."

Her eyes widened. "I—"

"Miss Cavanaugh is one of the prettiest ladies I've ever seen."

His sister gasped, and he smiled. "Do not be

dramatic," he admonished lightly. "I can admire a stunning jewel without coveting it."

She flushed. "Please do not seek an introduction! Keep your admiration at a distance. I would not be able to bear mother's upset nerves when the gossip rags mention it!" said Selina reprovingly. "She is without a dowry or any important connections. It is rumored her father lives abroad with a mistress and bastards! Who could ever align with such a scandalous family is beyond me."

Christopher pressed a kiss to his sister's cheek and extricated himself from her matchmaking clutches. Both his sisters had pleaded with him to attend, and far as he was concerned, he'd done his duty. It was not in him to dance with anyone tonight or deflect the sly flirtatious hints from those who wished to be a duchess. He had appeared to soothe their ruffled nerves. His gaze cut once more to Miss Cavanaugh who spoke to a woman who looked remarkably like her, only slenderer in her carriage. Her mother he assumed. The ladies conferred with their heads close together. The older lady swayed, pressing a hand to her lips in evident distress. No doubt the actions of Mr. Nigel Williamsfield had been imparted.

The ladies made their way through the crowd, and not wanting to be too obvious and incite speculation, Christopher removed his regard from Miss Cavanaugh and headed away from the crush toward the hallway. Instead of calling for the carriage, he went through the door opened by the butler.

It was still early, barely midnight. Several carriages were queuing, one carriage drawing away as one pulled up still delivering guests. The chilly night washed over Christopher, and he strolled past the line of carriages, apart from the revelry. Oddly, Miss Cavanaugh lingered on his mind. Had her carriage been brought around? He hadn't seen her in the hallway or outside on the steps. Had she snuck into the gardens with her mother?

He was confident Miss Cavanaugh had not recognized him as the Duke of Carlyle, for she had not descended into the usual tricks many young ladies of society tried to employ, hoping to compromise him into marriage. Miss Cavanaugh had been positioned primly to cry foul and bring down the scrutiny of society upon their heads. That was one of the reasons he'd remained silent upon her entry. Christopher had been secure in his anonymity in the shadowed corner of the library and had been confident she would not stay long. Then Nigel had entered and revealed himself to be the worst of cads.

How brave and proud she had been in her response to the man's betrayal. There had been no swooning fits, no pots of watering tears, no desperate pleas that he was her hope, nor had she tried to fling herself at him. Her reaction had been one of quiet dignity, and for the first time in years, he had found his interest captivated by a young lady of the *ton*.

When she'd let down her guard, dissolved into heartbreaking tears and curses, his interest had soared.

Now, what to do about it? Surely, after never feeling such curiosity or admiration for another on such a fleeting encounter, it bore study? He smiled at his whimsy. He navigated the dangerous waters of high society with effortless finesse born from years of practice. Christopher had avoided the mouse traps set by many maters of the *ton*. It wasn't that he had no wish to marry. Far from it. A duchess and children were inevitable. He knew his duty. It was the same of all previous dukes in his family. To continue their rich legacy, secure an heir, keep the family fortunes intact, and keep their name scandal-free.

These lessons had been imprinted in his mind and heart from when he was a lad of four years, sitting atop his father's shoulders as they strode through the apple orchards. From an early age, he'd understood the pride and prestige of his line and appreciated all that would be required of him once he became of age.

He'd been the 9th duke of Carlyle for the last four years, and he had done his most damn to uphold all the expectations of his prestigious title. Except for one. He hadn't married. All previous dukes had been wedded by six and twenty, and their heir and spare had been in the nursery by eight and twenty. The expectation was that he would marry a genteel, privileged lady without a hint of scandal to her name —a proper duchess who would set examples for the other ladies of society on proper etiquette and decorum.

At thirty years of age, he was still a bachelor with no prospect for a duchess on the horizon. His mother was beside herself, his sisters were adamant to fix this discrepancy, and he was...well contented with the situation. Only because he hadn't found *her*. Once he'd said that to his good friend Edward, the Marquess of Bancroft and the man had stared at him stupidly and declared all women were the same. Soft thighs and bosom to cradle a man and offer him sweet intimacy. All liked needlework, balls, and gossips. And if he spoke to one lady, he conversed with them all.

Christopher disagreed. Yet he wasn't altogether sure exactly what he looked for in his future duchess. The idea of someone as strict and proper as the previous duchesses was unappealing to him. While he was honor bound not to embarrass his title, he wanted someone he would like...admire...feel desire for, not a paragon of icy civilities like his mother and grandmother. Dear God, he loved them dearly, but no. And he wanted something more than admiration and lust, a rigidness to duty and decorum, but since he'd never experienced it before, it was undefinable. He believed when he found her, he would know.

His friends thought him an idiot for having such a belief. And after years of avoiding the marriage-minded maters, for the briefest while, a few moments past when he'd stared at the stranger's blotched tear-stained face. Something unknown had quickened in him and had silently asked the question...*is it you?*

The ball and the revelry behind him, he turned onto St. James's Street making his way to his townhouse on Grosvenor street. For the first time in his life, the question had stirred, and it was for a woman his mother and family would never approve for him. He smiled, genuinely wondering.

Is it you Miss Pippa Cavanaugh?

CHAPTER 3

"I fear we are ruined, my dear," Lady Lavinia Cavanaugh said with a deep melancholy sigh. "Nigel was your *only* chance." Before leaning forward to pick up her quill and sheaf of paper, the Baroness patted her elegantly coiffed hair to ensure nary a strand was out of place and smoothed down her ivory silk day dress at the front. Her mother always hid her hurt well by ensuring her mode of dress was impeccable.

"You are beautiful, mamma," Pippa said with a soft smile.

Her mother nodded, and a pleased flush had lent some color to her cheeks. For the last three days, she had been wan and listless.

"Our only hope now is to write to your father's heir, Mr. Winston Bellamy. He is unwed, and a pleasant young man. He's a second cousin so an attachment between you two would not be frowned upon. I'm certain I can direct his interest toward your charms."

Pippa lowered the book she'd been reading onto her lap. "Mamma, please. We have each other, and if we keep practicing sound economy, we shall be quite fine."

Light gray eyes a replica of her own settled on her. "Nigel courted you for several months, Pippa. He made promises to you...to me, and now this is what we are greeted with today." She slapped the newspaper on the small walnut table between them. "How are we to ever recover from this? How can I not do everything to prepare for your future when you are ruined?"

"There was no public announcement of an attachment between us, mamma," Pippa said patiently though her mother was fully aware. "There will be no scandal. Only disappointment and dashed hopes on our part." She thought of the stranger, the only other person who knew that there had been some expectations. Surely, he would not tell a soul. The man had not seemed a person prone to gossip and speculation. "But we will rally and press onward. I am certain the way is not to write to papa's heir."

Another heavy sigh from her mother settled in the room. Then she said, "Another letter came for you."

Pain and joy in equal measure rolled through Pippa. "May I have it?" she asked quietly.

Her mother plucked a letter from the stack of

correspondence before her and handed it to Pippa. She quickly grabbed a letter cutter and sliced open the seal.

Dearest Pippa,
How I grieve to learn of the difficult circumstances of the estates. Unfortunately, I am not in a position to send funds at this moment. My dear Anna is with child again—

Pippa flinched, her fingers clenching and crumpling the paper. Unable to read anymore, she folded it and slipped it into the pocket of her dress.

"What does it say?"

She snapped her gaze to her mother. In all the letters she'd ever received, not once had her mother queried their content. Pippa had been the stubborn one to impart specific news of her father. "Mamma—"

"I know you, my dear. You made a request for money...money that he can only get from his harlot." A fretful pause ensued, and her mother resolutely held her regard. "What does your father say?"

Pippa flushed. "He regrets that he cannot help."

Her mother flinched before bravely lifting her chin. "I will find a solution—"

"No mamma! I will find a way for us. Please let me share the burden. Will you attend Viscountess Shaw's ball tonight?" she asked hoping to divert her mother away from today's woes. Though Pippa feared they would be the woes of tomorrow and years to come.

Her father did not share their burden and completely absolved himself of all responsibilities toward his wife and daughter in England. He only cared about his dearest Anna and their children, and it had never been more evident. She'd written a heartfelt plea, outlining their dire circumstance without whitewashing anything, and he'd still refused. Her heart ached with a fierceness that almost made her cry.

Are we so insignificant to you, papa?

Pippa wondered if in America, where he lived, his children were branded as bastards, or did he pretend to be married to his Anna? How did he live with himself? And how she resented that she still cared for him and hoped his family was not ostracized.

"You are still a coward, Papa," she whispered, hating the tears that smarted behind her lids.

This burden to provide for their future now rested on her shoulders. Her mamma needed her to be strong, and inventive. They could not rely on the goodwill of the countess forever, and they would have to return to Crandleforth soon. They'd already retrenched, and a few servants had been let go to everyone's distress. The thirty-room manor with its extensive ground was taken care of by a very loyal skeleton staff. With their coffers running on empty, and tenants unable to pay an increase on rent, Pippa needed a wealthy husband who would not mind she came without a dowry and a past scandal, or she could seek employment.

It spoke volumes that employment was more appealing to Pippa. The notion would horrify her mother's sensibilities, but she could potentially earn enough money to ensure they were fed and clothed. Two gentlemen, and she used the honorific loosely, whom she had relied on had so easily betrayed the trust she'd given them. It was time to forge a path using her wits and intelligence.

She closed her eyes, hating the desperate fear worming through her heart.

The countess entered the sitting room, her cheerful manners preceding her like sunshine.

"Lavinia dear, how morose you appear this morning! Come we cannot have that. Shall we take tea together?"

Her mother brightened, and Pippa's heart eased to see it. She greeted the countess, and conversation on the latest gossip in the ton ensued. Pippa excused herself and hurried up the winding stairs and went to her chamber. Once there, she knelt and drew a small trunk from beneath her bed. She opened it and removed several bound books. Pushing to her feet, she opened the first book which had been smartly written by her.

Misadventures in Crandleforth.

A piquant story of a girl of eighteen falling in love with a young naval captain. The young girl had dressed as a boy to join him on his adventures, with much hilarity and adventures ensuing, with the promise of love between the pages.

With a sigh, she plucked at the list of noteworthy publishers she'd made a list of. "Courage," she whispered to herself. "All it takes is courage."

Jane Austen had published several works, and the world had seemed pleased when the author had revealed herself to be a woman. Pippa gently ran her finger across the name she had scrawled under the title.

Written by Phillip Cradmore.

Perhaps she could have it replaced by Pippa Cavanaugh. With a light laugh at her fancy, she closed the book, forming a plan in her heart. She would approach every publisher on her list until she found a place for her stories.

She recalled an advert she had seen from a popular printing press seeking writers. They would receive a visit as well. And if they were not interested, she would extend her search even further. It was time for her to take on the burdens of taking care of her future.

I'll not fail you, mamma. I vow it.

A FEW DAYS LATER, Pippa had almost given up hope. Several publishers had been reluctant even to accept her manuscript and give it a read because she was a woman. Their attitude had frustrated her, and even a few had asked her to reveal the identity behind the dark hat and veil she wore to each meeting. Of course, she had refused and had informed them only the written promise of a contract could motivate her toward that endeavor. Instead, she'd introduced herself as Miss Beaver, for having quite admired that animal for some time now.

But now, the press which had advertised seeking writers seemed quite interested, and she was dizzy with excitement and trying her best not to raise her hopes for them to be deflated. A portly man sat before her, a large oak desk separating them as he thumbed through her work. At times he paused, seemingly holding his breath, other times he laughed out loud, uncaring the author was before him, watching his every reaction with keen anticipation, and half dread and half thrill bursting in her heart.

He'd been reading for more than an hour, and she'd only interjected once to inform Mr. Bell that she drew inspiration from Shakespeare and Jane Austen, and that her blend of romance, adventure, and intrigue would appeal to the public given this year's bestselling books. Then, Pippa had contentedly sat on the edge of the well-padded chair, assessing every nuance of Mr. Bell's expression, at times shifting in her seat to peer at the section which caused him to chuckle so.

Finally, he set down the manuscript, and settled back in his chair, crossing his hands in a clasp around his rotund belly. There was a smile around his lips, and his amiable face did seem flushed with excitement.

"By jove, you have a talent, Miss Beaver. A wonderful, *wonderful* talent."

She barely prevented herself from bouncing on the chair. "Oh thank you, Mr. Bell, I promise—"

He held up his hand, and she faltered.

"I can see that you are familiar with the workings of upper society. Your rich description of the ball young Hetty attended in disguise was simply superb. The manners and etiquette conveyed in the viscountess's speech and actions are excellent. I simply cannot credit that to anyone's imagination. You, my dear, are a gentlewoman."

Pippa blinked. "Errr.... I have been privileged to be invited into certain circles before," she edged cautiously. "But I am not of the *ton*."

Mr. Bell considered with a good deal of skepticism before saying, "That will do if that is all you'll allow!"

Confusion bubbled inside her. "Mr. Bell, would you like to publish my story?"

He considered her for another second, then said, "No."

Her heart sank like a stone to the bottom of the ocean.

"But I would like to hire you," he said with a small, expectant smile.

Pippa stared at him all astonished. "*Hire* me?"

"Yes." The man nodded eagerly, a glint appearing

in his hazel eyes. "I am not currently seeking books and will not be for some time. But I am aiming to take the tattle section of my company to the next level. The public is eager, quite keen to read about happenings of the upper echelons. Gossip is what they care about! Not books. They hunger for stories such as the Worsley scandal and Sir Richards's afflictions. The public wants to read about their betters, about how flawed they are just like us regular folks. We want to know who is granting favors to rakes, who is running away to Gretna Green, who is marrying the footman and having an affair with the butler! The public wants the glitter—the parties, the shenanigans at masquerade balls, the fashion stars, and *faux pas*—and we also want the dirt. You are in a prime position to be the authoress of this tattling, Miss Beaver, and I will pay you handsomely for each story."

Pippa stared at the man, beyond intrigued, the promise of handsome pay an allure. And to be the author of society's scandal. The shame of it all! And also, the excitement she reluctantly conceded.

"How handsomely, Mr. Bell?" she asked for she could not forget how dire their finances were, and how melancholy her mother had been. For all intents and purposes, she'd already lost her father and might never see him again. Pippa could not afford to lose her mother too.

"I will pay you a pound and five shilling for every story."

She drew herself up in the chair, lifting her chin. "You insult me, sir, with such a paltry offer."

His owlish eyes blinked. "Two pounds."

She sniffed disdainfully. "No less than ten pounds for each article I write."

Mr. Bell spluttered. "Absolutely not," he barked, assessing her with shrewd eyes. "Five pounds and not a penny more."

Her heart was trembling with tentative hope, she held out her gloved hands. "Agreed. I want our agreement in writing, and I will only take bank notes, not a deposit. And with popularity, I shall expect a notable increase in pay."

"Agreed, Miss Beaver," he said skeptically as if he suspected that was not her real identity. "I will, of course, teach you about journalistic integrity and all the tricks of the trade to protect your sources and reputation."

He waited, drumming his fingers atop his desk.

"What tricks of the trade?"

This was a signal to bound from behind his desk, open the door and holler for a Miss Tilby. A few moments later, a woman of indeterminable years entered the office. She was dressed in a dark blue serviceable gown with a stiff collar. Her hair was pinned in a severe chignon, but it did not diminish the prettiness of her features. Instead, it highlighted her beauty. It was a pity her lips were so flat and unsmiling, and her brilliant green eyes so carefully guarded.

"Miss Tilby, please inform Miss Beaver who will be writing for us as..."

They both stared at her. She'd only thought of the one alias, but now she needed a moniker for the assumed name, *well...ah!*

"Lady W," Pippa politely murmured. It was simple and mysterious, and it would indeed pique her interest to read an article signed with such a name. "I will pen my tattles as Lady W, and you may refer to me as such going forward."

Miss Tilby's eyes widened. "A genuine lady?" she asked, a bit skeptically.

Mr. Bell nodded happily. "Please inform Lady W of the necessary tricks of the trade. It will take gumption to learn them."

Miss Tilby folded her arms beneath generous bosoms. "You'll learn to dress like a lad and blend in with the crowd."

Pippa gasped, an odd sort of excitement traveling through her. "Dress in trousers?"

"Yes," said Mr. Bell with a smug smile. "It is easier to pass unnoticed as a boy when following someone for a story. Did you read of the affair Earl Dunham had with the governess while his wife was in confinement? It was Miss Tilby here who got that story and broke it, and she did it dressed as a lad."

Pippa stared at her with newfound respect. "But you are a *lady*."

Finally, Miss Tilby smiled. "That I am. I am also a darn good reporter. But it is hard for me to get the latest *ondits* as seeing I am not invited to certain places."

Pippa stood clasping her hands before her. "What else will you teach me?"

Miss Tilby canted her head and assessed Pippa. "You'll be taught how to pick a lock. Loose-lipped servants will become your best sources, and with a few coins here and there, they will happily tell you their masters' and mistresses' business."

A startled laugh escaped Pippa. Surely, they jested. But she could see from the expressions they were entirely serious. "And this falls in the realm of journalistic integrity?"

"Yes," they said in unison.

Pippa was astonished, impressed, *and* excited. "How often would a story be required?"

"At least once a week," Mr. Bell said.

"There may not be a scandal every week," she murmured thoughtfully.

"But there can be a story," Miss Tilby replied. "The latest fashion and hairstyles. We could hint of engagements and speculate on attachments before such news are even broken to the *Times, The Morning Post,* and the *Gazette*."

"Exactly," Mr. Bell beamed. "People will gobble up the variety and be on tenterhooks for the next scandal."

Mr. Bell was ambitious in his comparisons.

Twenty pounds a month would go a long way in providing for herself and mamma. Even if it would not allow them to live in the style and comfort befitting a baroness and her daughter. But it was a start, and one Pippa would take. She knew of society's insatiable desire for scandal. She devoured the weekly penny sheets that told of all and sundry. And now she would be more than a purveyor, but an authoress. Trepidation and anticipation blossomed through Pippa, but she had to temper it with good sense. "I'll not pander to ruining anyone, Mr. Bell."

He and Miss Tilby shared a glance.

"My personal humiliation has been aired in scandal sheets across the capital before."

A shocked silence descended.

"My life...my mother's life became fodder for gossip and speculation, and for weeks we were dissected without remorse." She cleared her throat. "I would not be able to do that to another person."

Miss Tilby stepped forward. "Not every gossip is a scandal or a pathway for entertainment. We will respect your boundaries."

She assessed the pair. No nerve or uncertainty stirred within her belly. They seemed sincere, and both exuded integrity and pride in their work. This would be her first place of employment, and she was, in a sense, in dire need of it. But it was vital for her to feel at ease within the environment she would work. Holding out her hand to Miss Tilby for an unorthodox handshake, she said, "Teach me everything."

CHAPTER 4

Three months later...

"I declare I would give all my hat money to know the identity of Lady W," Miss Henrietta Rawlings said in admiring tones. "I daresay she must be someone of influence to know so much! Why, she'd declared puce feathered hats would become the rage, and it has!"

"I say she is a nosey body which should not at all be admired," countered Lady Amelia with a prim sniff. "And she must be one of *us* to know all she does, and why, that is insupportable."

Pippa sipped her glass of punch, hiding a secret smile. The very people who still treated her with veiled disdain had no notion she was the noted gossip columnist who was praised for her sarcastic wit, the quality of her stories, and frequently, satire mentioning some social injustice. At times, Pippa thought it all so absurd, but Mr. Bell had been true to his word. With each story written and delivered, she'd gotten a note of five pounds. In a couple of months, she'll have saved one hundred pounds, a small fortune in its own right. She could only anticipate what another year or two of savings could accomplish for her family.

Of course, not all her stories bordered on salacious. In addition to reporting on the elopements and the lovers seen scurrying off in dark corners, she also speculated on high profile marriages of members within the *ton*. A few weeks ago, she played a guessing game with the Marchioness of Brampton's son. To the delight of the purveyors of her scandal sheet, Pippa had declared the marchioness's son's name would be George, Elliot, or William. How surprised she'd been that bets had started at White's, and when the marchioness named her son George. The public adored Lady W even if she was unconventional in her scandalous tales. Such as, when she'd heard a countess scathingly remark that the orphans who accosted her carriages when about town should be flogged. Pippa had done a piece highlighting their desperate plight and asking for compassion instead of disdain. Mr. Bell had been surprised, but he'd allowed the article to be published. She'd done a follow-up, seeking donations for several charities and the response from the public had been incredible. Still, she was careful in also sating their insatiable appetite for tittle-tattle.

Her friendship with Miranda and the generosity

of their hostess Lady Leighton had seen Pippa attending many balls and routs. Though she found it uncomfortable integrating with a set who did not seem inclined to forget the terrible scandal or to be welcoming to her. It suited her purpose not to be popular or well sought after. That way, she was invisible to society, and surely no one would ever imagine her to be the notorious columnist.

"Oh, I do wish we were at Lady Burrell's weekend garden party instead. I heard that the Duke of Carlyle will be in attendance," Miss Rawlings continued.

Pippa gasped silently. Though none of the ladies would notice her behind the column which she stood. The Duke of Carlyle was loved by the public, so any story about him enticed the people. And with him being the catch of this season, she could only imagine the many scandalous situations that would occur or could give rise to speculations at the weekend-long event. Miranda and her mother had gone to that impromptu weekend garden party hosted by Countess Burrell. Pippa had thought it would be a dreadful bore to be holed up inside for a few days, mingling with people she could barely tolerate, merely because they resented her presence. But the duke's attendance would have made it worthwhile if only she had known.

"It's a wonder the duke would attend," Lady Amelia said with great disapproval. "Everyone knows a house party is designed for scandalous trysts! He is so very proper, and wonderful even if he can be quite terse at times. Why, I heard he made Miss Charmaine Gentles flee in tears a few weeks ago?"

"Do tell," another voice twittered.

There was a shuffle as if they huddle closer together.

"No one knows what happened, but she has declared her intention to avoid Carlyle at all cost."

"*Nothing* could induce me to avoid him! He is the most eligible catch for the last two seasons, and every mater would simply adore having a man of such wealth and consequences to be their son-in-law."

Several longing sighs sounded.

Pippa peeked around the column at that declaration and spied Miss Lucinda Brockman sighing over the duke. Pippa considered if there was anything newsworthy in their idle chatter to publish, or if she could inform mamma, she was ready to depart. Perhaps one story for the month about that particular duke was more than enough. She'd already mentioned a tidbit she'd heard a few weeks ago about the duke being affianced to a Russian heiress with more than one hundred thousand pounds a year.

She'd penned that little tattle of a engagement, and Mr. Bell had praised her for days. His paper that day had sold in record numbers as everyone seemed happy to wonder if their favorite duke might be hunting an heiress of immense wealth and unblemished breeding and reputation.

She had done her research and had not found

much printed about Carlyle beyond humanitarian motions he supported in parliament, and the articles of support he penned to whichever causes he lent his credibility and reputation. He was seemingly loved by all of society, the rich, and the downtrodden.

No hint of scandal had been printed. Well, none that Pippa found. And that had surprised her considering the Duke of Carlyle seemed well spoken of by society. A man of his reputation should have one or two skeletons, surely.

Despite attending quite a few events for the season, Pippa had never met the duke. The rumors mentioned he had no time for frivolities, so he hardly appeared at any society functions, of which she could attest. Since she was unlikely to be asked to dance or take a stroll about the room, Pippa sought out her mother, and a few minutes later they departed the ball without the story Pippa had hoped for tonight.

A FEW DAYS LATER, having just returned from another ball where she'd spied Lady Dunwood sneaking into the gardens with a known libertine. Pippa had started penning her story before even undressing from her gown, for Lady Dunwood was married to a marquess.

Lady W reports seeing a Lady D sneaking into the garden with Percival Gooden, at Lady Kasterlee's ball...

Pippa paused tapping the quill on the desk impatiently. She was always careful not to be too evident in the names she mentioned in her tattle sheet, not wanting to lead anyone to ruin, but to create a stir of speculation and fodder to feed the throng. At times she crossed Mr. Bell with her refusal to be too specific, but he was quite happy with the sales of his gossip column since she had started working for him and did not grumble too much. His sheets were touted as golden, and many speculated that the ever-increasing famous Lady W was a member of the upper set of society. How it thrilled the consuming public to know that such a possibility existed. Rumor already abounded that there were bets at White's about the author's identity.

She dipped her quill into the ink pot only to release it as if she had been singed when her door shoved open without the courtesy of a knock.

"Miranda, you are home! What has happened?" Pippa asked, hurriedly shoving the sheaf of paper into the upper drawer of her writing desk. Despite their close friendship, she had not confided to Miranda of her Lady W identity.

Miranda covered her face with her hands, her blonde ringlets shaking with her distress. "Oh, Pi... Pi...Pippa, I've been such a fool!"

"Please Miranda, dry your tears and speak clearly," Pippa cried, frightened by the copious amount of water work her dear friend shed.

"Something dreadful has happened over the

weekend at Lady Burrell's garden party, oh what a fool I've been!"

She hurried over to her friend, clasped her by the shoulder and led her to the bed where they lowered themselves onto it. "Dear Miranda, please tell me what it is so I may help you." *And I'll help you*, she vowed, owing much to her friend for the kindness she and her family showed to Pippa and her mother these last few months. "What is it?"

"I fear I am ruined," Miranda whispered.

Ice congealed in Pippa's heart. *Ruined?* Miranda was the most sensible girl she knew. How was this possible? "I don't believe it!" declared Pippa, trembling with indignation.

Surely, no libertine had been foolish enough to turn their rakish charms on the daughter of Earl Leighton and then abandoned her. "Please let me see your face," Pippa whispered.

Miranda lowered her hands, and took a bracing breath, before lifting her gaze to Pippa's. Miranda's eyes were vast pools of pain and shame, and Pippa almost cried.

"What happened?"

"Promise you'll not tell a soul," her friend whispered. "Vow it as we've vowed to be friends and sisters forever."

Unease shifted through Pippa. "But the Earl and countess must surely know too—"

"No! Mamma and Papa cannot know. Surely I would be banished to the country."

"Or they may force this bounder to do the honorable thing!"

Miranda's lips pinched. "He has no honor. No heart. And no character. How deceived I was of his nature. I declare mamma and papa would not be able to sway such a man any more than I did."

She gripped her friend's hand and cradled them between hers. "Tell me."

"Vow it first," Miranda cried.

Pippa nodded. "I vow I shall keep your confidence."

"It...it was the Duke of Carlyle. He has used and embarrassed me most abominably."

"The Duke of Carlyle!" There must be some mistake. But if dear sweet Miranda who is far too good-natured to abuse people has named the duke as a libertine of the first order, there must be some truth to the matter. "What has he done?"

Miranda's lips trembled. "Oh, Pippa. I...we were in a room together. *Alone*. I...I was bared to him. He saw me *naked* and has refused to make me an offer."

Shock almost felled Pippa, and she dropped Miranda's hand. "Naked? No shift or chemise?"

A flush burned Miranda's face bright red. "Yes," she said in a hushed whisper. "He has seen things... only a husband should see, and he has refused to see mamma and papa. In fact, he laughed."

"Oh, the heartless cretin!" Pippa could not credit he would act with such dishonor. Everyone thought the duke a dreadful bore. He was...spotless, his reputation unblemished by scandal. He was even mockingly referred to as the Duke of Saints. And he would do this?

Based on what she'd heard and read about the duke, she had never thought him a man with little regard for the conventions governing gentlemanly conduct. Admittedly, a gentleman would have offered marriage to Miranda immediately! But this ghastly beast merely took advantage of her innocence and left her to face the shame of her actions alone. What if someone had seen them together? What if he spoke about her dear friend as if she had been a conquest? Miranda would be irrefutably ruined. Worse, the shame she must be feeling now to have been so vulnerable before the duke to have him act with such rank dishonor. "He is abominable," she said softly, her heart breaking for her friend.

"I fear he has deceived all of society of his true nature," Miranda said on a sob. "I cannot credit he would act so callously...that he would discard me without a hint of caring for my reputation."

Pippa stood and strolled toward the fire, hating the chill worming its way through her entire heart. Were there no honorable men? Her Papa, Nigel, and the Duke were sterling examples of what a gentleman ought not to be! Yet their dastardly facets were hidden from society. No one knew her father lived in sin and had children out of wedlock. No one knew Nigel made false promises and now he was wed to an heiress. And now the duke...a man she had never met but had heard so many *honorable* things about was a cad and libertine! The injustice of it burned through her like molten lava.

"Miranda," Pippa said, facing her friend who remained huddled into herself.

"Yes?" she asked tremulously.

Pippa hated to ask, but she had to. "How...how did you end up in the room with the duke, naked?"

"Oh Pippa, I am mortified to reveal it."

"Did he force...force his attention on you? You must tell me."

Miranda closed her eyes as if pained. "Does it matter?"

"It does!"

"He did not force his regard, but I was led to believe we had something between us. He has treated me in the worst manner, and I am now ruined. I trusted in his reputation and his honor. I thought...I thought he might have feelings for me, but I was wrong. Oh, I cannot think or speak of it anymore, or I shall die!"

"Miranda—"

Miranda shook her head fiercely. "No. I collect you mean to reproach me, and I cannot bear it. Not from you, Pippa!"

Miranda launched from the bed and into her arms. They hugged fiercely. Pippa took a deep breath. "Might...might there be unforeseen consequences?"

They pulled apart and stared at each other.

"Whatever do you mean?"

Pippa blushed, vexed with her reaction when she wanted to remain unflappable for her friend. "Might there be a child?"

Miranda delicately cleared her throat. "Dear me no! We...I...nothing happened like in that book we read."

They both blushed, recalling the very naughty book they had mistakenly discovered in the earl's drawers and read. The content had been mortifying, and the words an education. They had hurriedly put it back and had been too embarrassed to discuss the material with each other.

"We must convince him to do the right thing," Pippa said with firm resolve. "I'll visit the duke—"

Miranda gripped her hand tightly. "He is unmoved by my pleas and desperation. He is the most unfeeling man! And I am ashamed when I think how I pleaded with him!"

Pippa stared at her helplessly. The situation called for more influential intervention, namely from Miranda's parents, the earl, and countess. "Miranda, you must consider informing your parents—"

"You promised," she said fiercely, tears pooling in her eyes. "Only you, the duke, and I know that I've been compromised and we shall keep it that way. I'll not die from it, but I'll learn not to be so stupid with my trust and affections ever again. Please, Pippa, do not betray my confidence. I just...I needed someone to speak to, I needed your shoulders to cry on."

Pippa nodded. "I promise you I shall make him pay for his repulsive behavior."

Miranda's eyes widened. "No, Pippa! Please do not approach the duke. You vowed not to tell anyone."

"I will not tell—"

"Please, Pippa. Let it go. I daresay it will take many months for me to look at the man and not swoon. But I must bear it and endure. He is powerful and very influential. His family is one of the oldest, and every mother wants him as a son-in-law. I do not want him to be an enemy of my papa, for he said he will not marry me no matter the cost, and I believed him," she ended on a sob.

Pippa hugged her once more, silently vowing to do away with the dastardly duke. The public adored and scrutinized the aristocracy and nobility, and that was how she would get the dratted man. As Lady W.

CHAPTER 5

An oddly placed sound in the night had Christopher lowering the paper he'd been reading on early experimentation with electricity. The riveting article was forgotten as another sound rode the air. He glanced to his left and stared at his windows. The scratching sound came from there. There was a nudge, a grunt, and he belatedly realized someone was attempting to break into his townhouse through the windows by the side gardens leading to his library.

The sheer shock of it flummoxed him for precious seconds. Who would dare?

A cold chill of warning darted through him. He fleetingly considered outing the gas lamp and plunging the library into darkness. The idea was dismissed, for though the blue and silver drapes covering the windows were quite heavy, the sudden dousing of the light might shed a different hue and alert the intruder. But he carefully turned down the wick until the library was painted in more shadows than anything else. Then he moved from behind the desk, collected the poker by the dying fire, and positioned himself by the wall of bookcase far from the windows, a place with more shadows than light.

The heavy drapes parted, and a small booted foot slipped through the window with surprising stealth. The other foot came, then the firmly rounded buttocks, and slim shoulders. The hair and features were hidden by a cap and a handkerchief, which was tied around the intruder's lower mouth and knotted at the nape.

The intruder glanced around the room carefully, his gaze lingering within the dark pockets. Christopher could sense the nervousness of the lad. The burglar moved with impressive stealth over to his desk, opened the drawers and carefully searched the contents.

Christopher's heart jerked when the intruder picked up his book of erotic drawings. The pages were flipped open, and a breathy audible gasp rode the air. A sound which he'd heard a few weeks past, had been hearing in his head ever since, and now replacing every gasp he would hear. He knew what had been seen. That first page had a lady splayed on a divan, and a man knelt before her with his mouth pressed to her quim. The erotic drawings were done by him, and it was not something he made public.

Instead of putting it back, a few more pages were skimmed.

It was slammed shut with such speed he almost chuckled. But he raised an eyebrow when the boy slowly opened it back - peeking at another drawing, and then several more.

Why was this person in his study...looking at his erotic drawings? Another audible gasp echoed in the room, and he could all but feel the young boy's blush and mortification. That book held some of Christopher's most lustful fantasies, some realized, and others were hungry dark urges he would wish to sate one day. Preferably with his duchess.

Taking another deep breath, the boy put back the book. A quick search of the other drawers revealed nothing, and the boy even took the time to glance at the article Christopher had been reading. It was interesting it did not seem as if he looked for money or valuables.

The intruder glanced about the room, his regard stopping on the ongoing chess game displayed before the sofa. He went over and bent low, assessing the placement of each piece. His clothing drew taut about his derriere as a delightful aroma filled Christopher's nostrils. This wasn't a boy. Only an imbecile would believe that those lovely curves, and that fragrant scent of roses belonged to a young man. It was not in him to define a woman solely by her physical charms, but Christopher would never in his lifetime forget that delectable backside—round, lush, pert, one of a kind, and he swore edible, and the breathy sounds of her gasps. After all, they'd been his companion for several weeks.

His intrepid burglar was Miss Pippa Cavanaugh. Or so the delightfully curved backside declared. He needed to confirm immediately, but he would have to tread with care. This smacked of a looming scandal of the unrecoverable type. And he felt protective of the damn, stupid girl. Her actions overwhelmed the bounds of propriety. Why would she take such a risk with a reputation already damaged?

She bent even lower, her lush backside arching even more. The handkerchief slipped, revealing the elegant curve to her jaw, the jut of her pointy chin, and those succulent lips. It was indeed Pippa Cavanaugh! A brutal shock of arousal arrowed through his body. Christopher swallowed. He hadn't taken a lover in more than a year, but still, the quick reaction of his cock as if he were a randy lad was unpardonable. Mastering his response, he smiled without humor. It would serve her right if he kissed her senseless before the night was out.

"Oh, how clever!" she cried softly shifting to assess the board from another angle. "I wonder who your partner is. Each play is equally brilliant."

With a low chuckle, he leaned the poker on the bookcase and stepped silently closer to her.

What she would do when he revealed himself, he could not anticipate. And he was almost startled by the mild amusement rushing through him. A slow curl of desire sped through his gut, hardening his length. He could ravish her here and now, and the world would be none the wiser.

Foolish, Miss Cavanaugh. Utterly silly and reckless.

***

"I PLAY MYSELF," a voice drawled.

Pippa froze, the brilliance of the chess match forgotten. She didn't dare breathe. She *couldn't* breathe. The voice belonged to the duke! For no other would have a chess set in the library. Why was he at home? All research had said he would have been at his club, a place he visited every Tuesday evening for port and cigars with his cronies.

Bracing herself resolutely, she straightened and faced the voice. The sound of booted feet drifted closer, and her heart beat with such fright she almost fainted. Pippa could not believe, on her first-midnight adventure she'd been caught. Miss Tilby who'd become her friend and mentor would be sorely disappointed.

Pippa was painfully aware she was alone with the man in his home. Rumors said he lived as a bachelor at his opulent townhouse, for his mother, the Duchess, had her own lavish abode in St. James's Square. Pippa was frozen, trying her best to find the appropriate excuse. What would he believe?

"I believe I am in the wrong house," she said with

low huskiness, desperately hoping to disguise that she was a lady.

The man's approach faltered, and she all but felt his amusement.

"So you meant to thieve from someone else, did you?"

"I'm not a thief," she snapped indignantly, an odd shame burning through her.

"Just a burglar? Now, why does that make little to no sense?"

She frowned at the familiar tones.

The wick of the lamp was turned up, bathing the library in a bright, warm glow. She gasped as his features were revealed. "You!" she cried before she caught herself. She was so astonished that for a full minute she could only stare at him, her thoughts mush.

"Oh?" A mocking brow was arched. "Do we know each other?"

"Of course not," she hurriedly said.

Her midnight stranger and the duke were the same, a circumstance which she regarded with mixed feelings. How could this man who had been so kind to her, despite the wickedness which had glowed in his eyes, be the one to seduce and discard Miranda callously?

"Who are you and why are you in my home?" he demanded softly.

Pippa was scared and doing her best not to act rattled. He was not behaving as how one should upon discovering an intruder in their home. There was no evident anger, nor was he attacking her. No cavalry had been called to make an arrest. And that scared her even more.

There was a tightness across her chest that made it difficult to breathe.

"I believe I shall take my leave," she said inching toward the way she came.

"I believe not," he returned smoothly, advancing on her. "I have all rights to keep you here, wouldn't you agree?"

How fiercely her heart trembled, and she felt ill. she weighed her words carefully before asking, "Will you have me arrested?"

If he did, there would be no recovery from the scandal. Pippa closed her eyes briefly. In her bid to seek revenge for her friend, she had placed her and her mother's future in jeopardy. Her hands shook, and she took deep breaths to prevent herself from throwing up. *Oh, what am I to do?*

He considered her for several moments then waved his hand toward the chess set. "Play with me," he invited. "I've not had a challenger since my father died, and you seem as if you understand the game."

His words set her heart to pounding, for it had been the same with her. Only her father had been an equal player and a lover of the strategic game. She wanted to have nothing in common with the wretched duke, but she was also very wary of refusing him. "Your Grace—"

"Play with me, and you'll escape the jail. Perhaps you'll even be inspired to say what you wanted from my home, hmm?"

She stared at him from below the cap helplessly. For a wild moment, she wondered if she revealed her identity if he would be more lenient. *Do not be foolish!* She berated herself sharply. Under no circumstance could he know his intruder was her. And she would need to tread with the utmost care in extricating herself from this situation. Pippa owned that she could be headstrong, and too impetuous, and now she had been caught! This was beyond the pale. For now, she would have to be the piper to any tune he demanded. "If I play with you...you'll not have me arrested?"

He dipped his head, and a small smile touched his mouth.

"And I'll be able to leave freely?"

He canted his head with arrogance. "If you win."

"And if I should lose?"

"You'll owe me a boon."

Swallowing nervously, Pippa padded around the chest set and lowered herself to the floor, folding her legs beneath her. The duke lowered himself as well before the pieces, and it was then she saw his state of undress. A blush heated her face to note the muscles of his arms for his sleeves had been rolled to the elbows. His feet were bare, and he only wore a white shirt tucked into his trousers. There was no cravat, and she could see the strong muscles of his throat.

Dear God, if she kept blushing, no matter how she kept her head down and her voice low, he would know she was a lady!

"A drink?"

It was then she noted the glasses and a decanter of amber liquid in his hand. When had he gotten them? She considered refusing but found herself saying gruffly to deepen her voice more. "That would be pleasant."

A half smile touched his lips, and she narrowed her eyes beneath the cap. Did he suspect that she was not a boy? It was far too taxing on her nerves to try to understand what was happening.

Amber liquid splashed into the glass, and he held it out to her. She took it and tentatively sipped. It was the same liquor as the last time, so she was better prepared to handle the hot slide of the whisky down her throat.

"Let's play," the duke said with evident pleasure.

She assessed the board keenly and the moves which had been made. Her style was one of patience, but she saw an opportunity which she could explore. She moved a pawn to capture his pawn, strengthening her control of the board's center. The duke smiled, his hand darting with speed to claim her pawn with another pawn, balancing the power in the board's center. His strategy was decisive ruthlessness, while hers was of deep contemplation, of plotting her moves and his ahead by several steps.

At times he sent her quick smiles of admiration which warmed her insides.

"You are an excellent player," he praised. "I declare I am glad you broke into my library."

A shock went through her, hot and delicious. Pippa gripped her glass of whisky, needing an anchor against the invitation to banter in his eyes. She lifted the glass to her lips, and with one long swallow finished the fiery drink, her gaze never leaving his.

He paused, reaching behind him for something. He lit a cheroot, bending his dark head and cupping his hands over the flame. He dragged long into his lungs and exhaled from his nose, curling smoke around them. She liked the smell of it, and she subtly inhaled secretly titillated. She'd never seen a gentleman smoke before. They'd always hidden away with their ports and cigars. It was a bit of a disappointment to know that it was not more of a ceremony.

He held it out to her. "Smoke?"

Pippa almost fainted. "No."

"I won't tell if you won't."

The familiar phrase sent her heart to pound in its fiercest beat since he'd revealed himself.

After a half-hearted attempt to convince herself it was too improper, she reached for the cheroot. It felt so delightfully wicked to indulge in something so simple. Pippa belatedly realized she should have been finding out things with which she could ruin the duke, or blackmail him into doing right by Miranda, but she was enjoying the freedom of not being so proper and perfect as dictated by society.

She inhaled quickly and regretted it immediately. The smoke burned her throat, and she dissolved into a fit of coughing which transformed into choked laughter.

"Your first time?" he asked with devilry dancing in his eyes.

Of course, he knew! "Yes, and while it is excessively diverting, I do not believe I shall try it again," she uttered, furiously aware of flaming cheeks.

They played for several minutes, before he said, "What kind of burglar are you? I saw no interest in the candlesticks or monies I had in my drawer."

Her fingers paused on the bishop. There was a short silence, broken only by her ragged breathing. "What kind of man has a dual reputation?"

He stiffened perceptibly. "Do tell."

She shivered at the dark throb of warning in his tone. "You are the Duke of Saints are you not? That is what many in society call you. I am sure you are aware of your moniker. Yet you have a book...that is decidedly not *saintly*."

Dear God, she needed to find a way to control these urges to blush. Her entire body felt too warm recollecting the wicked, wicked images. The awareness of how alone they were seeped into the air.

He reached for his glass and tipped it to his lips. "A most extraordinary thief. Your intimate knowledge of me says you are familiar with the *ton*."

She lifted a shoulder in a deliberately casual shrug. "I read the scandal sheets with the best of them."

"Even more curious. An educated thief. My interest is snared."

Drat! To avoid responding she swallowed the remainder of her drink, distantly realizing this was her second glass, and she felt...tingly and hot, and there were butterflies in her belly.

This is dangerous. The knowledge slammed into her with the power of a careening carriage. She swayed before catching herself. Pippa lifted her gaze from the board, and the predatory gleam in his eyes had her faltering into stillness. Waves of shock and tension poured through her. "You know I'm a girl," she said huskily. "That is why you've not called for help!"

CHAPTER 6

The duke's sensual lips curved in a small smile. He reached out and touched her chin with a finger. That slight touch felt like a carnal assault on her senses. Pippa felt his touch through the handkerchief—an unmistakable possessive caress she did not understand. She regarded him speechlessly. Something impossibly heated slid through her veins.

His bright silver eyes burned with desire, and her body trembled in reaction to the knowledge. *He plans to ravish me.* A strange stirring began in the pit of her stomach and drifted lower. She felt as if she were falling...endlessly into a moment she did not understand but wanted. Pippa had never felt like this in all her years, and she slid an accusing stare at the empty glass still clutched in her hand. *It must be the whisky.*

Pippa did not like the way his stare riveted on her. His intention pulsed in the air around them. She

MISADVENTURES WITH THE DUKE

leaned away from the intimate caress, and he lowered his hand. She tugged the cap lower, hiding her face. "I cannot stay," she whispered, settling the glass on the carpet. This had to be handled with care lest she trapped herself in a situation wholly unfamiliar to her. Games of seduction and temptation were not known to Pippa.

A decidedly imperious brow rose. "Our game is not over."

"I can tell that you want to kiss me!" she burst out. So much for handling the matter with delicacy. It was impossible to pretend ignorance and now was not the time to be naïve. She felt frightened...and also tempted. Many nights she had wondered about the stranger who had offered his brand of comfort and had pulled a smile from her when her heart had been numb with pain.

"I want to...desperately."

Her mouth dried. *I want to kiss you too*. She shook her head, fighting the awakening realization. Pippa feared she was on the verge of doing something truly stupid. She searched for a clever and witty response but could not find her tongue. She cautiously lifted her head and peered upward at his impenetrable mien. "Your Grace—"

"You broke into my house, we are drinking and smoking together. I daresay you may call me Christopher."

She took a shuddering breath. "You may call me... Miss Beaver."

He chuckled, the sound low, deep, and frightfully appealing. She inched away from him.

"You have nothing to worry about, Miss Beaver. I do not take unless I've been offered, no matter how tempting your plump lips are."

"I must beg of you to guard your tongue!" Lest he tempted her to irresponsible wickedness.

He reached out and tugged the handkerchief down to her neck. She lowered her head, so the cap would hide her face from full view. His thumb stroked along her jaw, and then her chin, and her heart rate tripled as he caressed the side of her neck. This was wrong, so wrong, and yet...her lips parted.

The loveliest breeze glided through the open library window, cooling the odd heat fluttering in her stomach. She glanced desperately at the clock above the mantle. "We've been playing over an hour, Your Grace...Christopher. And I predict we have several more hours to go to end this match. I...I cannot stay until dawn."

"I will let you go...if you promise to finish this game with me."

He asked the impossible, yet something wild burned inside her to say yes. "I will think on it."

"I will accept that for now."

She pushed to her feet, hurrying to the windows.

"I shall escort you to your carriage."

She glanced over her shoulders, regarding him with some amusement. "You believe I took a carriage to infiltrate your home?"

He looked enquiringly across at her. "I've seen odder situations. Allow me to escort you to your equipage."

"I walked."

"You must live nearby then," he murmured, watching her keenly. "Have we met? You seem familiar."

Why did she feel as if he mocked her? Was it possible he knew her identity? Pippa suspected that he was merely amusing himself at her expense and was mischievously enjoying her discomfiture. She was amply disguised, and they had only met once, and that was three months ago. Yet, Pippa could still recall with startling clarity every detail of their first encounter in Lady Peregrine's library. *What if...* "No, we've not met."

"Please, take the front door. And I shall walk with you until you are safe."

Panic beat in her breast. "I am obliged to you, but it is quite unnecessary, I assure you!"

"I insist," he said in a tone of tolerant amusement. "All sorts of dastardly elements walk the streets at these hours. Even Grosvenor Square has hopeful footpads lurking at these hours."

Unable to think of any suitable rejoinder, she ignored him and slipped through the windows before he could protest, lightly running along the footpath to the side gate. Once away from his townhouse, she felt relieved. Pippa glanced around, hating that the duke had been correct. Even though the area was so fashionable, it could be dangerous. She had to walk a reasonable distance before a hackney carriage could make itself present. Keeping her head low she hurried forward on to Brook Street. Home was in Russell Square and would be at least a half hour walk.

The deliberate click of a cane on cobbled steps had her whirling around. Her heart sank. It was the duke. Dual needs of relief and trepidation clutched at her heart. If he followed her, he would uncover her address. Conversely, she felt decidedly safe to have him with her. There was a nip in the air, and with a querulous sigh, she tugged the cap lower over her head, wishing she had worn more than the tweed jacket borrowed from Miss Tilby.

They walked in silence for several minutes, and her thoughts considered how to disguise her abode. Miss Tilby lived in a most modest area, and if Pippa ventured there, she would be forced to spend the night. How would she explain that to mamma? Pippa had been at Lady Grayson's ball, and she'd complained of a headache to return home. When her mother had wanted to accompany her, Pippa had insisted she stayed and enjoyed the ball.

They turned left onto Hanover Square and then right onto Princes Street. A young boy loomed ahead, and he had the roughest look. She inched closer to the duke, and she could feel his amusement. But she was grateful for his company and suddenly furious with herself for the risk she had taken. Though she had intended to only be in his home for a few minutes and not over an hour!

"Thank you," she said softly.

He shot her a look of undisguised surprise. "What have I done?"

"Many other gentlemen would have called the runners or magistrates to collect me. Instead, you gave me a night of experiences unlike any I've ever had and will cherish."

She kept her head down, but she felt his stare as it touched on her.

"Take off the cap and let me see your face," he murmured.

Pippa laughed lightly. "I shan't, and I do not believe you truly expect it of me."

The boy approached, and Pippa stiffened. He was older than she'd first thought, his face was covered with soot and a touch of desperation. The duke stepped forward, cutting him off from being too close to her. His protective gesture warmed her, and she peered at him.

What she saw was a kindness so rare, for a second, she doubted its genuineness. The duke was shrugging from his coat. When he was free of it, he handed it to the lad. Instead of appearing grateful for protection from the cold night and the slight drizzle of rain, the boy assessed the material critically, no doubt considering its worth. The duke said something to him, and the boy stared. The duke also handed him something she could not see, but when the boy flicked it, she discerned a sovereign.

Then the boy hurried on.

"Why did you give him your coat and money?"

"He was cold, and perhaps hungry. The money is an advance for working in my stables."

This astonished her. "He works for you!"

"No, but if he is interested, he will start tomorrow."

She absorbed this in startled silence. *Who was this man?* "So, you can be compassionate."

"You say this as if you know me to be cruel and callous, my intrepid thief."

"No," she murmured. "I have no experience with the manner of your character."

She glanced in the direction the lad had disappeared. Even if that boy sold the coat, and he would be smart if he did, food would be in his belly and his family for several weeks from the profit. It was a kind thing the duke had done, and acknowledging it, shook Pippa. In her experience, those who were selfish users did not have the withal to perform acts of charity and kindness. She was tempted to believe in what she saw, but she could not let the dratted man deceive her of his true character. Beneath the heart of the charming, fascinating man tonight was the morals of a snake!

The clip-clop of hooves had her glancing down the street. How fortunate! A Hackney was delivering someone home. The duke generously hailed the man for her, and she made her way to the small carriage.

"Thank you," she said, careful to keep her features shadowed by the hat.

"Until we meet again," the duke said, sounding very confident it would happen. Then he paid the driver and stepped back.

She glanced at the driver. "I will inform you of where to take me when we are away."

The small rotund man shot her a curious stare before shrugging as if to say whatever she wished. She hopped into the carriage, genuinely appreciating the freedom trousers provided. The carriage rumbled away, and she opened the small window and shouted her address to the coach driver.

Several minutes later, Pippa snuck into the countess's townhouse, grateful to see everyone was still at Lady Grayson's ball. She hurried to her room, ripping the hat from her head as soon as she made it inside. One thought had dominated her musings on the quick ride over. The duke wanted to kiss her...and she had ached for him to do it.

Recall what he did to Miranda, Pippa reminded herself fiercely as she jumped onto her bed with a gusty sigh. The man is not to be trusted. Yet the feelings in her heart did not want to listen to her logical mind. *Who are you...and why do I want to know you?*

Quite irritated with herself, she scrambled from the bed and hurried over to her small writing desk, grabbing a small lamp from the mantle as she went by. Opening the drawer, she retrieved a sheaf of paper, quill, and an inkwell.

> *The Duke of C is a jaded libertine, and not all society believes him to be. A rake of the first order, a man scandalous in his musings and deeds hides amongst society, a dangerous wolf...a jackal in sheep's clothing. This author has it on the first most authority he is not to be trusted, he is a man with little honor and no regard for the innocent, and he shamelessly seduced a fine, wonderful girl at a particular garden party a few weeks ago and then refused to marry her.*
>
> *He is a wicked, unprincipled libertine...a dangerous wretch. All young ladies of virtue should steer clear!*

Taking a deep breath, Pippa wrote every reason she should not trust the duke or allow her foolish heart to be compromised. She must redeem Miranda's honor. Pippa could not fight a duel on her behalf, nor did she have the power to disrupt his business and investments. But this she could do, warn other unsuspecting debutantes of his vile, wicked, and rakish behavior.

And I must keep my heart and reputation intact while I do it.

With a sigh, she glanced down at the writing in her hand, knowing she would not be able to publish it. For though Miranda was her friend, Pippa hadn't witnessed his dastardly deed first-hand, so she needed evidence to corroborate Miranda's painting of his character. Which Pippa had failed to do tonight. All she'd confirmed was the duplicity of the man. She folded the paper neatly and slipped it between her diary. Instead, she drew another sheet and recalled the scandalous drawings she had seen in his book.

A blush heated her cheeks. Pushing down the flutters in her heart and the peculiar heat in her belly, she started to write.

A duke by any other name! This author...

CHAPTER 7

A duke by any other name! Touted as honorable, and a sterling example all young bucks should emulate. This author has it on the highest authority that a certain duke is nothing but a libertine who believes his lovers should be spanked. Grab your weekly features of the tattle to keep abreast with the Duke of Disgrace.

There were only a handful of dukes within society, and most were old and doddering. Only two other dukes were within his age, but it was he, Carlyle, those other young men were often urged to emulate. But the most heart-pounding fact was he had sensually spanked his lovers in the past. How many other dukes in society had such sexual urges and predilections they kept ruthlessly hidden as he did with his desires?

And how would this author—he glanced down at the signature—Lady W be privy to it? Worse, it was by sheer bloody chance, the headline which screamed Duke of Disgrace caught his attention. He did not live his life by chance or happenstance. His days and evenings were carefully planned and inked into a calendar, so there were no errors, no breaches in expectations, no possibility of scandal. It was the least he could do. For his father and his forefathers before, whose reputation had been the bedrock of their motto.

Duty and honor above all.

Another glaring fact he could not ignore: Miss Pippa Cavanaugh had seen his book of erotic drawings. Might it be that she had informed this Lady W of the explicit and lusty images? Was it that Miss Cavanaugh was prone to gossip and revealed their encounter? Christopher frowned. That assessment felt wrong. She had been so nervous he hadn't the heart to inform her he knew her identity. He'd allowed her the disguise, charmed by her bravery, and delighted by her skill in playing chess. It was unlikely this woman would dare tell anyone she had been improper and broken into his home and found the scandalous drawings. The only other conclusion he could reasonably draw was that Miss Cavanaugh and Lady W were the same.

A far reach, but so probable. Astonished, he read the article once more. *Duke of Disgrace.* He couldn't decide if he should admire her audacity or punish her for it. Society would be in a frenzy to figure out which particular duke this gossip spoke about.

Another awareness flowered through him. If she was Lady W, she hadn't broken into his home for silver, but for dirt and secrets. A cold chill of warning sliced through him. Did the foolish woman want him for an enemy?

The door to the breakfast room opened, and his mother sailed inside.

"Christopher, I see you have forgotten we were to meet today?"

His mother was gravely dignified and implacably garbed in black, her mane of golden hair piled high on her head. And had always been that way as long as he could remember. She sat beside him and lifted an imperious chin to the hovering footman, who hurried over to pour her tea. After taking a sip, she shifted her regard to Christopher and smiled her greeting. Of course, she wouldn't have kissed his cheek or touched his hand briefly. There had never been messy hugs from her or brushing kisses on his cuts when he'd hurt himself from playing. Yet he knew she had loved him with her entire heart. Just in a dignified, duchess like manner.

"I seem to have forgotten. What meeting?"

She arched an elegant brow. "Why to discuss the list of course."

This arrested his attention wholly, and he folded the pressed paper and rested it beside his cup of coffee. "An investment list?"

"Do not be silly. The list of eligible ladies this season suitable for a union with our family."

"Mother, I am not familiar with this list," he murmured mystifyingly, though he'd suspected from her militant carriage.

She shot him a birdlike look of inquiry. "Oh? I thought Selina had informed you we would take a more active approach in the matter of finding you a duchess."

Bloody hell. "I see."

His mother smiled brightly, but her hazel eyes were hard and determined. "Yes, the girls and I met yesterday and we made a list of all the eligible young ladies this season. We referenced their dowries, and family connections and found seven girls who are just lovely, Christopher. I am sure you will be well pleased. Selina and I prefer Earl Rumford's daughter. Lady Elinor's carriage and comportment are that of a duchess. I daresay you will approve of the match."

He took a contemplative sip of his coffee. "Why is it so important to you that I marry now?"

His mother inhaled sharply. "You are Carlyle! Your dukedom is one of the most prestigious of this country. Not just anyone can be your duchess. She must be impeccable. It is your duty—"

"I know my duty," he interrupted gently. "My first memories of father were sitting atop his shoulders as he guided me to understand what it means to be a duke. I know what my responsibilities are to my tenants, the various estates, and my family. I appreciate the interest you take in my life. I love that you and Selina and Amelia care about my happiness. But I will choose my duchess when I am ready."

He didn't think there was anything he could have said to shock his mother more. Well, maybe if he admitted a perplexing interest in Pippa Cavanaugh. That interest though had to be paused indefinitely, until he found out exactly why he'd become a target for a scandal sheet. The dreams he'd had last night of kissing her senseless, of stripping her naked and worshipping at the altar of her generous curves, simply had to stop. It had been years since he'd pleasured himself, but lustful fantasies of Miss Cavanagh had urged him to take his cock in his hands last night with thoughts of her driving him to a powerful release.

"What nonsense are you saying, Christopher?"

He ruthlessly pushed Miss Cavanaugh from his mind. "I will choose my own duchess," he repeated firmly. "And I hope you'll love her as I do, once I find her."

She dealt him an arrested stare. "*Love?*"

Her aghast tone implied his mother thought him an idiot. Christopher smiled without humor. "Love, admiration, respect, friendship. The things I would like to have with the lady I would ask to be my wife."

His mother closed her eyes briefly as if pained. "Dukes do not marry for love or admiration. Your wife will respect you of course," she said crisply, her eyes flashing with anger. "But this notion you have is nonsense. The last time you thought you loved someone, it was the most ridiculous and inopportune girl! You cannot be allowed to choose for yourself and disgrace our family!"

"And do you believe me to be that same boy of twenty years old?" he demanded with an arrogant tilt of his head.

Her lips flattened in a thin line. "Of course not. You are an exemplary man and duke as all previous dukes, and I simply want it to stay that way. To select your duchess without any suggestion from me and the girls cannot—"

"And yet that is what will happen. I am aware of my rank and position in this life, and the kind of woman needed to walk by my side. I'll not hear of it again, mother, nor will I tolerate any more matchmaking antics. My wife will be *my* choice, and you can rest assured I will not disrespect my position."

They stared at each other, and several moments passed before his mother sighed and nodded her agreement. His promise lingered in the room, and a knot formed in his gut. With such a promise, whatever fascination he'd been feeling for Miss Pippa Cavanaugh had to be suppressed. If he pursued her, he would be going against his position and family's expectations.

A mistress then, the crawling hunger in him suggested.

He cursed silently. She had seemed so proud and beautiful that night in the library, so clever and brave the night she'd broken into his home. She did not deserve to be a mistress because her father had proven himself to be a dishonorable cad. It was either he ignored her or strolled close enough to her flame to find out if she had the character worth fighting for —kindness, loyalty, faithfulness.

Is it you...?

And everything in him said yes, and he wanted to explore that. Because if it was her, he did not want their ships to pass each other. He almost shook his head at his romantic idiocy, a thing he'd never been prone to before. Christopher wasn't a man who believed in pure chance, but nor did he dismiss its possibilities. Things were either carefully plotted and executed, or they existed beyond his capability of control and simply had to happen. He believed in the tangibility of science and the whimsy of fate.

The fascination he'd been battling since that night at Lady Peregrine's ball, when Pippa Cavanaugh had stared at him with her large wounded, and yes, ugly splotched face, felt like whimsy...fate.

And he needed to find out the possible role she could play in his life. Lover, enemy, friend...or a duchess.

SEVERAL DAYS later Amelia invaded Christopher's study, slapping a scandal sheet atop his desk. "Is this you!" she cried, pointing at a section with a cartoon.

In it, the man had tied his cravat around a lady's

hand to what appeared to be a bedpost. Scandalous indeed, for the expression of the man implied he was a debaucher, while the young lady's appearance was one of tears and innocence. Bloody hell. He was almost anxious to read the damn article.

The duke of many knots, the headline screamed.

"Christopher?" his sister asked.

The man in the drawing bore no resemblance to himself, so he did not understand the fuss. Unless... his gaze dropped to the author. Ah, Lady W.

> *This author has it on the highest authority a certain duke has found another use for his cravats. And it is not to tie around his neck! Shocking and not so saintly one could say. Mothers should be mindful of their precious daughters who could be led to ruin by the duke of C.*

The blasted woman had penned at least two more inflammatory pieces over the last ten days, all featuring the duke of C, where only an idiot would not know it spoke of the Duke of Carlyle.

"There are only two dukes of C within society, and I doubt Carrington, a man I declare to be not a day under seventy is using his cravat to tie his lovers," his sister cried, a blush engulfing her entire tall, slender frame. "This Lady W's suggestion is outrageous and libelous, and she must be stopped! Mamma's nerves are shattered at the very suggestion this...this article may refer to you."

He carefully folded the article and leaned back in

his chair. "In case you hadn't notice, poppet, I have a guest," he said coolly.

Her hazel eyes, much like their mother's, widened in alarm at doing anything so improper, and she whirled around as the newly minted Viscount Shaw, Sebastian, rose to his feet. "Lady Blagrove," the man said with a smile. "A pleasure."

She nodded regally slightly bobbing the perfect blonde chignon at the nape of her neck and sent Christopher a look of censure passed down from mother to daughter as if to say why did he have the viscount in his home. Christopher silently chuckled when she huffed at the blank stare. The viscount was a genius with investments and a solid character which Christopher genuinely liked. The man had recently married a lady who had courted scandal by jilting the Marquess of Trent at the altar last year. Rumors claimed Fanny, Viscountess Shaw, had caught the marquess in a very salacious embrace with his mistress on the day he was to marry Fanny. Christopher didn't vilify the lady for running away from the bounder. Society had not been as kind or understanding, mainly since she then chose to marry a man who worked and owned factories.

Christopher liked and admired the couple and counted the viscount a friend. His sister's ridiculous prejudice would not change that fact, no matter how much he adored her. To society and his family, it was hard to accept that Viscount Shaw had not been born into their privileged life. He was a self-made man of great wealth who owned several iron smelteries. He did not belong, and they did not hesitate to remind him. But the viscount tolerated it all with some amusement, and his lack of ruffled feathers made Christopher admire the man more.

With a pointed look at the newssheet atop his desk, Amelia marched from the library.

Sebastian sent him a look of bald amusement. "I'd wondered if the articles referred to you."

Christopher arched an arrogant brow. "Do you read the scandal sheets now?"

The viscount chuckled. "My wife swears she is above it all, but she seems quite delighted with this Lady W and reads everything the woman writes. It seems Lady W has targeted you."

Christopher grunted, rising from behind his desk. "She has. I'd not wanted to rush to that conclusion, so I gave her a little time. Now there is no doubt confidential information gleaned from my home is being used to bring scrutiny to my name."

"How did this woman get your private information?"

"She broke into my library almost two weeks ago."

The glass of brandy making its way to the viscount's mouth froze. "The hell you say!"

"I do say it," he said on a light chuckle. "I believe it is time for me to ask the lady why she has targeted me." Dark, heady anticipation curled through his gut at the idea of seeing her again.

"You know her identity?" the viscount demanded after taking a healthy swallow of his drink.

There it went again, that odd need to protect Miss Cavanaugh. "I do, but I will not reveal it."

"Ah...you are protective of the lady, curious." Intense speculation glowed in the man eyes.

"Shall we return to the architectural plans Mr. Ashley has drawn for us?" Christopher asked, collecting several rolls of papers from his desk.

The viscount was ambitious enough to want better living conditions for the workers of his factories. Better homes with at least two rooms and a small parlor. Better latrines, and better health care. Many other factory owners resented him for his innovation, hating that many workers flocked to the viscount's employment, leaving the other owners behind. It had made the viscount many enemies, and he had thought it prudent to ask his powerful friends to weigh in on the housing crisis.

The one-bedroom hovels many of the workers lived in now spread many diseases and misery all around. The duke and the viscount were working together and buying up land across the city, and in several other areas, with the intention of developing numerous housing projects.

Since Christopher had gotten involved, he had taken over a few factories operated by unconscionable men. The conditions women and children worked in had been deplorable, and he hadn't been able to leave it be. He'd made them offers their greedy hearts could not have refused, and now he worked with the viscount to improve it all before he divested himself of it. Possibly he would sell them to the viscount himself. His mother had fainted when he'd told her of his interest in helping the workers of the factories. He'd obligingly spent the afternoon with her to soothe her nerves, but he would not be deterred from doing what was just and honorable.

He'd already written numerous arguments he would take to the house of Lords at the next sitting, addressing the need to improve workers' lives and prospects amidst the new wave of industrialism sweeping the country.

Their meeting resumed as if his sister had not interrupted, but it was all a carefully constructed façade of business for Christopher. Inside he was being eaten alive with the need to see Miss Cavanaugh once more. *Damn her.* This time, no matter if she proved an enemy or a friend, he would kiss her...endlessly. If only to verify that the reality of her was nothing like he had been ardently dreaming. Maybe then, he would be able to place Miss Cavanaugh into sharp and logical perspective.

CHAPTER 8

It had been a terribly long three weeks since the night Pippa broke into the duke's townhouse. She had not seen him in society since, but the wretched man lived in Pippa's mind, and nothing she did would remove him.

Lady Rutherford's midnight ball, an event Pippa had anticipated, was in full swing, and many daring ladies had been sneaking off to the gardens with known rakes, but Pippa had little interest in following for scandalous speculations. With a frustrated groan, she lifted the glass of champagne—her third—vowing to banish any warm, curious thoughts she had about the man.

Why do I think of you so much? He was a bounder, and she'd had her fill with trusting undeserving men and would not be foolish in leading her heart to pain and disappointment again. Still.... He'd given an expensive coat to a stranger. Could a bounder be so kind? He had escorted a thief to a hackney, paid her fare, and wished her a safe night. Most lords would have been so affronted, she would have probably spent the night in jail. Instead, they had played brilliant chess, drank whisky, smoked cigars, and chatted. And she'd wanted to kiss him...still did if she was being honest with her desires.

To what purpose?

Carlyle was in possession of great wealth and power, owning vast amounts of lands, tenants, and other properties. His reputation as it stood was spotless, despite her attacks. Society seemed to be in disbelief their saintly duke could be their current duke of speculation and controversy. If the Duke of Carlyle was interested in kissing a girl like her—as he had desperately claimed—it wasn't because he would take her to be his wife. Pippa was far too inferior for him to even consider the notion. So the dratted man would only toy with her as he had done Miranda.

And that awareness made her angry and disappointed. Pippa owned another had never occupied her mind and dreams in such a manner. A blush heated her entire body, and she glanced around to see if anyone stared at her oddly. She worried for naught, no one was interested in the daughter of a disgraced lord standing on the sidelines watching everyone else dance.

Somehow, she had to prevent a repeat of the last few nights' dream. She'd dreamed of one of the erotic images in the duke's book. The one where the lady had been wantonly splayed on a chaise and the man's face buried between her legs. But in Pippa's dream, it had been her and the duke! Hours later Pippa was still mortified the man had invaded her slumber in such a manner, and not once but thrice. Clearly, she had her father's lascivious and improper blood, and those who had whispered *'blood will tell,'* had not been too far off the mark.

Her mother, appearing quite radiant tonight in a red gown with a crossover bodice boasting gold stripes cut on the bias, slid up to her. Pippa was grateful for the distraction. The flush in her mother's cheek and the twinkle in her gray eyes were decidedly odd. Pippa stiffened when her mother cast a tender glance at Lord Janson, a widower who had only recently come out of mourning. Was he the reason her mother seemed so...happy? A smile touched the man's lips, and to Pippa's shock he winked...*winked* at her mother before turning away and heading out into the gardens.

Good heavens! What was happening? "Mamma?"

Her mother glanced at her, a silly smile painting her lips. "Yes, dear?"

"You're more energetic than usual today."

Her mother smiled wryly. "I have reason to be."

What did that mean? "Why was Viscount Janson...winking at you?"

Her mamma inhaled sharply, her cheeks blooming a delightful pink. "I'm sure I have no notion of what you speak." She snapped open her fan and started fanning herself.

Pippa had no idea what to say. But there was something there, those tender glances were not her imagination, and she'd developed a keen eye for these sorts of things. Worry curled through her. Mamma had been much devastated by her husband's betrayal, and she'd always seemed so vulnerable to Pippa. Now, this viscount showed an evident interest, and his intentions could not be honorable. Not when all of society knew that mamma was still married, and a divorce was impossible to secure. What if he wanted her to be his mistress? The very idea of her mother driven so low was heart-breaking. A fresh surge of anger and hurt at her father's action surged through her almost felling Pippa to her knees. "Mamma, please be careful," she beseeched softly.

The baroness stared at her for several moments before squeezing her hand. "Graham is very kind and understanding. Not every man is a bounder and deserving of your mistrust."

Oh dear, Graham? Pippa winced. How could mamma open her heart so easily after the man she had loved for over eighteen years betrayed her love and trust so horribly? "Mamma, please, promise me you shall be careful."

"The Duke of Carlyle, the Marchioness of Andrews, and the Countess of Blagrove," the butler announced.

Her heart lurched, and like many in the room, her

attention turned to the entrance of the grand ballroom as the duke was announced with his sisters. Nervousness coursed through Pippa. Since she'd invaded his privacy, she had dreaded meeting the duke socially. Would he recognize that she was the same as his thief?

"My, how handsome he is," her mother said appreciatively.

The duke was quite handsome indeed, dressed in dark trousers and jacket, snow white undershirt, a light blue waistcoat, and an immaculately tied cravat. Typical cut and style of clothing most fashionable gentlemen wore, but they fitted the duke's frame with uncommon grace.

Pippa glanced about searching for her friend and almost cried when she spied a stricken Miranda staring at the duke. She closed her eyes before hurrying through the open terrace doors to the gardens. No doubt she would stay there until it was time to depart. Pippa would offer to leave with her now. "Mamma, I see Miranda in the gardens. I will check on her."

The fan in her mother's hand fluttered wildly. "I believe he is coming toward us!"

"Who?" Pippa glanced around and almost expired. It was the duke...and he was indeed heading directly to her with the hostess. Her heart became a roar in her ears, and her skin crawled as the people's regard settled on her. He approached with their hostess, and Pippa was grateful for the sudden warmth of her mother who pressed closer to her.

"Miss Cavanaugh, His Grace, the Duke of Carlyle has asked for an introduction, and I am delighted to oblige," said Lady Rutherford the hostess of tonight's ball with curiosity alive in her brown eyes.

Struggling for equanimity, she ignored the thrill of excitement and the agony of nerves going through her veins. She dipped into an elegant curtsey quite aware of the shocked stares and the whispers already cresting through the ballroom. For once Pippa asked the same question as the throng, why had the duke approached her? Surely, he did not know? It was impossible. That night she had been in full disguise, and their first meeting had also been in a darkened library.

"Miss Cavanaugh, I'm delighted." He bowed charmingly before turning to her mother who tried to mask her astonishment and hope. "Lady Cavanaugh, how charming to make your acquaintance."

Her mother curtsied and returned a greeting. Mild pleasantries were exchanged with the hostess and mamma. Though the duke did not look in Pippa's direction, she could sense all his awareness was for her. She was unsure how to feel about his assessment. *Am I nervous or excited?* That question might remain unanswered of the night, she was only sure that the strange feelings flipping around in her stomach were because of his presence.

He turned to her, his eyes alight with warm

humor. "Miss Cavanaugh, I do hope you will honor me with a dance this evening."

Lady Rutherford froze, then twittered, "Your grace! I'm sure Miss Cavanaugh would be pleased to know this is your first dance of the season!"

The countess's staged whisper had several ladies snapping open their fans. The buzz of their murmurs and speculation crawled over Pippa's skin like ants.

She stared at him helplessly. "It would be my first dance of the season too," she murmured.

Lady Rutherford sent her a horrid stare as if Pippa should not have admitted no one had cared to stand up with her, even once. And perhaps she should have been more mindful with her tongue. Making a desperate recovery, she said, "All my dances are available."

Her mother inhaled sharply, and she blushed. *Drat*. It was as if all her lessons on proper interaction with a gentleman had flown through the open terraced windows.

"If I could take them all, I believe I would, Miss Cavanaugh."

His lips curved and an answering smile was irresistibly drawn from her.

The orchestra started a waltz, and he held out his hand. "If you would honor me now, I would be most pleased."

She threw a glance at her mother who merely stared with such wide eyes, and pitiful hope, Pippa almost burst into tears. She dipped into a curtsy, placed her gloved hand on his arms, and allowed him to escort her onto the ball floor.

The bows of the orchestra leaped to life, and the exquisite music of the waltz filled the room. He swept her into his arms with innate grace and elegance, and Pippa followed seamlessly. "I've never danced the waltz before," she murmured, feeling wonderfully awed.

Surprised flared in his eyes. "I would not have been able to tell. You move beautifully, Miss Cavanaugh."

A sweet, mystifying ache trembled low in her belly. "Thank you, Your Grace. My fa...father taught me." And the memories of her fifteen-year-old self, giggling and having great fun in her father's arms as he taught her the steps almost overwhelmed her.

Swallowing back the mess of emotions stirring in her heart, she smiled. "Thank you for asking me. I... I'm not asked to dance often." *Or at all*.

And the duke's attention tonight would go a far way in restoring her unfairly tarnished reputation and honor. A lump grew in her throat until she could barely swallow. She could see the happiness of her mother as she stared at them from the sidelines. A duke danced with her daughter. One who was well loved and respected. Pippa would not need many stamps of approval after that.

Surely, he knew he did her a great kindness.

"I did nothing but asked a lovely lady to dance with me."

His eyes glowed with wicked tenderness and distressing familiarity. A lump grew in her throat, and she looked beyond his shoulder, unable to stare in his face. *He knows it was me.* The awareness filled her, yet foolishly she was not afraid. "What you must think of me!"

"I admit you are the most fascinating creature I've ever met, Miss Cavanaugh. I have yet to decide if that is good or bad. Meet me at midnight in the gardens. That is about two hours from now," he murmured.

"Your Grace?" Pippa demanded wholly taken aback.

"I would like to continue our conversation and our game. It has been...haunting me."

A jolt of apprehension went through her at the confirmation he knew it had indeed been her inside his townhouse. The dark heat in his gaze and feminine awareness warned Pippa it was her who had been tormenting his thoughts. *Do you have wicked dreams of me too?*

Cynical humor entered his eyes. "No denial, I am impressed, Miss Cavanaugh. I had prepared for a volley of tears, vapors, and machinations."

"I would like to think I am a good deal more sensible than that." Though her anxiety was cramping her gut. She could not determine what he would do with the information. Pippa thought it unlikely he would pursue the matter lawfully, but it felt wretched to be so uncertain of his intention. She could deny it since there had been no witness, but it would be her words against a powerful duke.

"I gather to adopt the person of Lady W one would have to be. Even my sister Selina reads your articles, finding them clever and resourceful without being malicious. Amelia is not too fond, however."

Pippa stumbled but he held her securely in his arms, and only the keenest of observers would have noticed that slight mishap. It was impossible the duke would know that much. Fearful denial hovered on her lips. She had been careful of her secret identity. If society knew Pippa Cavanaugh, a lady already barely tolerated, was the source of their tattles, she and her mother would never be invited to another ball or drawing room. Everyone in society would cut them. "Your Grace, I—"

"There are far more interesting and scandalous people than me," he said, "Did you know Viscount Charleigh dresses as a woman and sings for others at a special club in Soho square?"

She choked on air, so outrageous was his suggestion.

The glint in his eyes said he funned her. "I would not tell a tattle that has the potential to ruin a life."

"How excessively diverting. A gossip columnist with integrity. I am in admiration," he said with chilling sarcasm.

She flushed. He tugged her scandalously close and turned her in to a spin. "I do not appreciate even the hint of my name in a tattle sheet. Why have you targeted me, Miss Cavanaugh?"

"Are you so uncaring of your misdeeds you had not thought it possible? Or are they so vast it is difficult for you to keep abreast of them?" She threw the accusation at him with a quick, disgusted narrowing of her eyes.

Curiosity flashed in his gaze. "Ah...this is revenge is it?"

"Yes," she snapped, thoroughly vexed with his cavalier attitude. "I shall occupy myself with the revelation of the true nature of your character until I am satisfied society is fully aware of it as well!"

"And what is the truth, Miss Cavanaugh?"

She ignored the cool warning in his tone, searching his expression for any hint of remorse or guilt. There was none, only a watching ruthlessness, characterizing the duke a man she needed to be careful with, a warning she did not heed. "That you are a libertine! A seducer of innocents, and that the Duke of Saints is a carefully cultivated persona that is no more factual that I am actually a widow called Lady W!"

Icy civility settled on his face. "And whom have I supposedly seduced?"

She glanced away recalling her vow. "I cannot say, but I am certain you are guilty!"

"Ah...and to think I'd believed you were different from the typical gossip monger."

A quizzically raised eyebrow brought blood rushing to her cheeks.

"If you dare repeat such a falsehood, I will sue you for slander."

The soft menace in his voice shocked her speechless. "This is not mere gossip. You hurt someone close to me, someone, who trusted you, someone who has taken me into her confidence of your dastardly nature!"

Only icy coldness peered down at her, and in his eyes, she saw ruination she'd not thought possible. This man would not allow serious scandal to touch his name without her facing the consequences of his power and connections. Intimidation pressed in on her, and she regretted she had ever wanted to kiss this deplorable blackguard.

"You will scarcely deny that you are acquainted with Lady Miranda Cheswick," she whispered fiercely, assessing every nuance of his expression.

CHAPTER 9

The duke stared at Pippa, arrested, his expression one of mild shock. "And what has she accused me of?" he demanded softly.

"I ought not to have said that. My wretched tongue!"

A cold, intimidating fire leaped into his eyes. "I ask you again, Miss Cavanaugh, what dastardly act am I meant to have done, to Lady Miranda, I presume?"

The disdainful slant of his lips inflamed Pippa's ire. "Only what you have done, surely you should know it!"

"You have a remarkably false notion of my character."

The waltz ended, and she was grateful, hardly knowing what to make of the man. The look of surprise in his eyes now seemed so genuine. But she knew her dear friend would not mistake the matter, would she? Pippa hated the doubt worming through her heart. She did trust Miranda, they were the best of friends. But why did the duke betray such surprise?

Only now, the eyes peering down at her were blank with icy civility. "You set out on a campaign of ruin without confirmation of this dastardly act. You are a silly, immature miss not worthy of my regard!"

Pippa flinched. She had felt suddenly breathless, and embarrassed, and perplexingly hurt.

The countess came up at that moment to tell Pippa that her mamma required her presence, preventing her from uttering the retort that rose to her lips. In silence, he escorted her toward her mother.

"This conversation is not over, Miss Cavanaugh. Nor is our game. I will see you at midnight."

"I thought I was unworthy of your regard?" she snapped.

"It seems as if I am a damned fool, for I want nothing more than to meet you."

That coldly biting acknowledgment infuriated him more. It occurred to her, despite his rank and position the duke was drawn to her. The notion did frightening things to her heart.

"You brought your chess board and pieces?" she asked, instead of denying the outrageousness of what he suggested and running far away as possible. She tried to reassure herself she was merely seeking ammunition for Miranda, but deep inside...Pippa was a mess of bewildering emotions.

He tapped his temple once. "We will play here."

She was momentarily diverted. A mental chess game, moving each piece from sheer memory? How positively thrilling. She remembered the last move she had made and each placement of the board with sharp acuity. "I will not promise to be there."

The duke spoke to her mother briefly before melting away into the crowd. Pippa was painfully aware of all the avid stares of confusion aimed her way because the duke had danced with no other. His sisters sent her several assessing glances from behind their fans, and she wanted to flee from it all. But she had never been a coward, and she would not start acting silly now. Lifting her chin, she made her way through the throng, searching for Miranda. Pippa was disappointed to learn her friend had pled a headache and departed while she and the duke danced.

It tore at her heart to know her friend could no longer enjoy a ball. She would not dare slip away to meet him in the gardens. Though, based on the kindness she'd gleaned from his character she might be able to convince him to do the honorable thing. It had been a few weeks since the dreadful incident, and some nights Miranda still cried herself to sleep. Pippa hated the wretched, hollow sounds that came from her friend's room.

Almost an hour before midnight, Pippa found herself discreetly slipping through the doors of the music room some distance away from the main ballroom, which led to a section of the outside gardens. A few lanterns along the pathway and on overhead strings lit the way, but the area was empty. A chill breeze danced over her, making her shiver, but she did not mind it. As she stared out into the swells and shadows of the gardens her heartbeat escalated to an uncomfortable speed. *I am being silly, I cannot take this risk.*

With a sigh, she turned around and slammed into a hard form. Shock sent prickles all over her body.

"I see you were just as anxious as me to begin our game," the duke said with some measure of amusement. "An hour early, Miss Cavanaugh?"

Her nostrils filled with the pleasant scents of tobacco, brandy, and the man himself. "I was about to return inside," she said with a scowl he would unlikely see for they were obscured in shadows. "I was foolish to come out here."

This felt too much like a romantic rendezvous.

There was no immediate response to this, but after a few moments, he said, "I wanted to dance with you again."

"I wish you weren't so provoking," she said in a hushed whisper.

"I only speak the truth, Miss Cavanaugh."

How coolly bemused he sounded. Then he said, "Rook takes e7 bishop."

Her heart leaped, the pieces of the board imprinting perfectly in her thoughts. "Bishop takes e4 knight," she murmured thoroughly thrilled with the dratted man.

"Smart," he praised, slipping his hand around her waist, and fitting her hand atop his shoulder before urging her to sway sensually to the waltz playing in the distance.

"Dancing and playing chess, Your Grace?" Yet she adored it all. *Oh, what am I doing?*

"I'm a man of numerous talents, Miss Cavanaugh."

She smiled briefly, ridiculously tempted to move closer to him. As if he sensed her scandalous thoughts, he tugged her closer, swaying her onto the softly padded grass. Her heart tripped with alarming pleasure. "And what else do you enjoy? Aside from playing chess...and dancing of course." *And ruining innocents.* Except that reminder felt hollow as if she did not really believe it.

"I like to draw."

She faltered in his arms completely, recalling the wicked erotic images. "You were the one who did the scandalous drawings?"

"Ah, I'd forgotten you'd peeked at those. How brave and naughty of you to ask, Miss Cavanaugh. Did you by chance think of them often my little thief?"

Her entire body blushed, and it was his turn to falter into astonishing stillness. She considered berating him for his improper remark but decided that it would be wiser to ignore his impertinence. "You are entirely wicked," she said, recalling the explicit nature of the pictures.

"Will you allow me to kiss you, Miss Cavanaugh?"

She gasped and stared up at him. *Yes!* But her logical heart said, "I cannot."

"A pity," he said with a rueful smile. "It would have been delightful."

It was then she recalled his promise that he would not take, only if she offered. She stared at him mutely, her heart a wonderful, beating mess. I've never been kissed before, she wanted to say. Miranda had laughed gaily while regaling her with tales of how many charming *beaux* had stolen a few kisses. At those lonely times, Pippa had felt a burst of envy. And now here was this man, a duke no less, staring at her with a naked hunger, as if he was not at all perturbed by desiring to kiss her. With a sigh, she leaned into him, and that was all the motivation he needed. A rough sound slipped from him, and he released her waist to frame her face with his hands, then took possession of her mouth.

It was a simple kiss, a brief exchange of breath, a brush of lips against hers, without demand. It was as if the duke waited for something and when Pippa did not respond, simply because she did not know what he waited for, he licked along the seam of her closed lips. Her lips parted on a soft gasp, and he kissed her with deeper intimacy. The first wicked taste of him was a shock against her senses. An inarticulate murmur slipped from her, and she glided her hand around his neck, thrusting her fingers through his hair.

He groaned his approval while wrapping his arms around her in a tight and possessive embrace.

He kissed her with gentle bites and nips, coaxing a wanton response, and she surrendered to his ravishing assault. It felt as if Pippa's world caught fire. Everything was heated...shockingly, carnal heat. The stroke of his tongue against hers jolted through her body, set her heart pounding, and heated the blood in her veins. He tasted of whisky and berries, and something heated and delicious. He tasted like sin... and passion...and adventure. He also tasted of ruin and pain. A whimper of denial passed from her mouth to his, and he swallowed the small soft noise.

The duke glided the tips of his fingers over her hips, and now to the curves of her thighs. A violent shock of heat tore through her when he gripped her buttocks. Pippa trembled.

She broke their kiss, breathing raggedly. "Your Gr...grace!" Her voice shook. Hunger, fear of the unknown, need and uncertainty, all rushed through her as he stroked his fingers over the swell of her backside. It was all so improper and wicked!

"Christopher," he murmured. "It would please me to hear my name on your lips...Pippa."

Was this how he'd been with Miranda, sweet, tender, and seductive? Pippa stiffened, and immediately he released her from his embrace and stepped back.

"What is it?"

She pressed a trembling hand to her lips. She

paused, and after considering for a moment, asked frankly, "Why did you kiss me?"

He created a wider space between them. "Forgive me, I acted in haste."

Shock jolted through her. An apology was the last thing she expected. "Your Grace?"

"You have no father or brother to defend your honor. I should not have allowed this...to traverse this path without an understanding."

The proper, saintly duke stood before her, his expression hooded. Yet a few moments ago he had kissed her with a burning passion. Those explicit touches without the benefit of courtship had been from the depraved duke, and it was he she wanted in front of her, speaking with only honesty. But what did she want him to admit? That the feelings crawling through her body were the same he'd felt, and that he hungered for her with similar ferocity?

"I will visit your mother in the morning," he said stiffly as his eyes darkened with unnamed emotions.

"To do what?" she asked all astonished. Then awareness dawned. "To declare yourself...because you kissed me?"

He tilted his head.

Incredulity filled her. "I am two and twenty, and this was my very first kiss. I've had no stolen moments most other young ladies giggle about, for no gentleman saw or desired me. Only the scandal of my past mattered. Only my lack of connections and dowry mattered in determining my worth. So I thank you for the experience, Your Grace. I was surprised... by how wonderful it felt. I was appalled at myself for wanting to kiss you...forever. But I daresay I will not run screaming into the night that you had compromised me and demand that you marry me. Also, *I* wanted your kiss, or I assure you, Your Grace, I would never have allowed it." A very bold and honest speech except she had ruined all her worldly assurances with her furious blushing. Pippa wanted to crawl under the garden bench and hide from her silly and girlish reaction.

And then inexplicably she knew this man had not seduced her friend. *What happened, Miranda?*

"Then I bid you good evening, Miss Cavanaugh. We must finish our game some other time, if at all," he said with reserved indifference. "I cannot leave you out here alone, so if you will precede me inside?" Then he waved along the path behind her.

Pippa smoothed down her dress and patted the chignon, ensuring all was in place. "Good evening, Your Grace," she said softly, hating the ache in her chest. She wanted nothing from him or any man. So why did she feel so wretched?

It was because he sounded as if he had said goodbye, as if he saw the kiss as a ruinous mistake, as if he was no longer interested in their chess game, as if she were no longer interesting. Turning around, she hurried inside, hoping to leave the desperate ache for more behind her in the darkened gardens. Having any hopes in regard to the duke was silly.

It would be beyond foolish to allow her heart to become entangled with a man so above her in circumstances and expectations. A man whom her dear friend had set her cap at. But the terrible ache in her heart followed her all the way to the countess's townhouse, and into bed. And even when she hugged the pillow and prayed to stop thinking of the duke, she dreamt of him—doing far more wicked deeds than kissing.

CHAPTER 10

The Duke of C titillatingly danced only with one Miss C at last night's ball. Is this a blossoming romance in the air? Or is the duke taking pity on a particular lady no young bucks have asked to dance all season? This author declares...

Christopher lowered the newssheet with a small smile. *Clever, Miss Cavanaugh.* And he understood why she had done it, even though the article brought unneeded attention to her. Lady W had been diligent in reporting all the latest tidbit. It would have been inflammatory and suspicious if she had failed to report on the duke of C dancing with Miss P. Christopher found the *ton* and their insatiable appetite for gossip simply ludicrous, even if amusing at times.

Dismissing the scandal sheet and vexed with the amount of time he had given those newspapers this week, he went back to the reports detailing the performance of the railways as an effective means of transportation in the cities of Birmingham, Liverpool, and Bristol. The idea to lay tracks across the entire country was innovatively ambitious, and he supported the movement wholeheartedly and contributed significantly to the private capital funding that built the rails. More funds were needed, and it would take some time to assess how precisely the spending committee planned to utilize the thousands of pounds he would invest.

A pair of light gray eyes darkened with passion crowded his thoughts. With a sigh, he released the sheaf of papers and leaned back in the chair. *By God, I will excise the taste of your lips from my damn mind.* A thing he had been vowing to do for the last few days. Except he genuinely did not want to. But he didn't want Miss Cavanaugh to be such a distraction either. In the four days since he last saw her, memories of dancing, kissing, and playing chess with her teased him in the days, then taunted him mercilessly at nights. *Do I haunt you as you've been haunting me, Miss Cavanaugh?* Her lips had been so soft and yielding to his kisses. The feel of her lush backside had been the sweetest torture. He wanted to do such wicked things to her lips, and that pert rump. He wanted to see it blush a pretty red when he sensually spanked her, then nibbled. He hungered to see those curves arched lasciviously while he urged her to her knees and elbows and sank his cock into what he knew would be sublime tightness.

An odd recognition blossomed through his heart. He was a man of experience, but he'd never felt like this before...ever, and he doubted he could ever feel this way again. The desire befuddled him. He truly wanted Miss Cavanaugh, but the intensity of it unnerved him merely because he never imagined another could consume his thoughts and desires in such a manner.

He needed to make a firm decision in what capacity he would pursue Miss Cavanaugh. Christopher chuckled, wondering if she would be open to his advances. The manner in which she had returned his kiss said yes, but there had been a shadow in her eyes he'd not expected. She had been hurt before and was rightfully skittish. And he knew the two men who had gravely disappointed her. Had there been others?

A knock sounded on the door, and he pushed aside his musings of Miss Cavanaugh. The butler came into the room and bowed. "I beg Your Grace's pardon; your grandmother has called. She awaits you in the gardens."

His family had apparently called in reinforcement. No doubt the latest mentions of the Duke of C had driven them into an apoplectic fit. She had been at his country estate in Dorset these last several months, not interested in visiting London for the season. His grandmother was even more proper and exacting than his mother, but it had always been easier speaking with her. What he would say to her was another matter? "I will be with her shortly. Have tea and cakes brought to us."

The butler bowed again and withdrew.

A few moments later, he strolled toward his grandmother, his two wolfhounds—Astra and Samson—bounding playfully by his side. They had been gifts from his grandmother who would never admit her deep love for dogs. Even now she would barely pat their heads, for it was too unbecoming to lower to her haunches and greet them with hugs.

She stood as he approached, a woman not yet seventy who remarkably appeared several years younger, with barely a touch of gray in her rich dark mane of hair or wrinkles on her skin.

"Grandmother," he greeted warmly, dipping to press a kiss to her cheek.

She eyed him critically, and he grinned. "Do I pass muster?"

A smile twitched at her lips, and she lowered herself to the stone bench. He sat beside her, ignoring her disdainful sniff when the dogs sprawled at their feet. They exchanged mild pleasantries before she got to the heart of what had driven her from the country.

"I've heard a most alarming rumor, and this news reached me in Dorset."

"I am certain you exaggerate the importance of whatever you heard. Those country folks believe a lady smiling in the presence of a gentleman is news."

"Do not act facetious with me, Carlyle."

She insisted on calling him by his damn title, and nothing he said would deter her, for referring to him thus was proper. "And what shocking titbit have you heard?"

"You've danced only *once* this season...and it is with the most unsuitable girl."

"Ah, it relates to Miss Pippa Cavanaugh. Important then."

His grandmother shifted, glaring at him with silver eyes a perfect replica of his own. "This is true?"

As if his mother and sisters had not given her an earful. "It is," he said with a slight dip of his head.

"Do you understand the speculations surrounding both of your names because you singled her out for your attention? My dear boy, the matter must be rectified immediately."

"I will," he promised. "My intentions will become clear, and there will be no need for speculation by society."

She gasped before freezing in evident astonishment. "Your intentions?" she queried through bloodless lips as her eyes narrowed.

He smiled gently, wondering who in their right mind would want to marry into his overbearingly pompous family. "Yes," he said fondly scratching behind Samson's ear. "I plan to woo her...and make her my duchess if she will have me."

His grandmother actually spluttered. "If she will have *you*? You, my dear boy, are Carlyle! If she will have you? What outrageousness is this? If I should ever condescend to approve the match, she will be a duchess, and you doubt she will have you? Who is this gel?"

He tipped his head to the bright sky squinting against the fiery ache of the sun, thinking through Miss Cavanaugh and her exciting complexities. "She does not see me as a duke, but as a man," he murmured. "I do not think she cares if I am wealthy or a pauper, but it does seem to matter to her that I am kind."

The memory of the admiration in her eyes when he'd given the boy the coat floated through him, along with the pain and condemnation when she thought he'd been dishonorable. "Her trust has been betrayed before, but it has not made her bitter or spiteful. She is refreshingly honest and seems to possess no skills for flirtation or artful flattery. Miss Cavanaugh is loyal to those she calls a friend even to her own detriment. A lifelong companion with such qualities is more precious than rubies. I will not allow our ships to sail past each other."

His grandmother gasped softly at his crudeness. "That bad business with that gypsy girl—"

He stroked along Samson's back, allowing icy civility to creep into his tone. "I am no longer a boy of twenty. And that gypsy girl died trying to give birth to your grandchild. She had not been a mistake, but an experience I will never regret. I only wish her life had not been lost."

"My dear boy—"

He leaned in and kissed her cheek before standing. " I trust I can rely on you to convey your approval of my choice when I make it to mamma, Selina, and Amelia."

She harrumphed, and he grinned. "Shall we retire inside so I may read Dickens's latest masterpiece to you?"

With a sigh, she nodded, and he assisted her to her feet. The dogs bounded after them as they strolled along the cobbled path to the side entrance of the townhouse.

"Tell me more of this Miss Cavanaugh," she invited.

And he did. Describing her lovely smile, the way she worried her bottom lips when she was anxious, and the fierceness with which her eyes sometimes flashed. Belatedly, he realized he spent an inordinate amount of time talking about her eyes. After a while, it occurred to him his grandmother meant for him to speak of Miss Cavanaugh's family connections and her reputation. He fell in to silence quite perturbed by the poetry he'd been waxing. To feel so much for a lady who might not regard him even as a friend was distinctly uncomfortable.

They entered the house and made their way to the smaller sitting room.

"Take her to be your mistress and be discreet

about it," his grandmother murmured sitting on a well-padded high back chair and peering up at him. "I can tell you are smitten, maybe even more, and will not let go the idea of her. Set her up and never let your duchess find out and be careful not to foist any bastard on her."

"Before I knew Miss Cavanaugh's identity her strength and dignity captivated me. Her ability to laugh despite wounds carelessly dealt to her heart revealed much about her character. Her adventurous and improper spirit bewitched me. And she is the only woman I can recall since I've inherited the dukedom to speak to me with honesty, whether it be in disdain or admiration."

With each softly placed word, his grandmother's eyes grew more rounded, and her fingers dug more into the armrest.

"The only position a woman such as Miss Cavanaugh deserves in my life is that of my duchess or a respected friend. I will not marry a lady for more power and connections. Never that. I take the time to explain this, Grandmother, not because I need your approval, but because I respect and love you. Do you understand?"

Oddly, the eyes peering up at him glowed with love and admiration. "I do."

"Good." And he finally felt at least someone in his family understood his position. His wife would be his choice. And right now his heart and mind leaned toward Miss Pippa Cavanaugh. Christopher simply had to determine now if she felt the same way.

A FEW DAYS LATER, Christopher alighted from the carriage which had taken him to Croydon, to the estate of his good friend the Marquess of Bancroft, only an hour's drive from London. The man had planned a day party comprising of archery, blind man's bluff, cribbage, and a picnic. This was a yearly event hosted mid-season by the marquess, and it was well attended by the fashionable ladies and gentlemen of the season. The marquess's manor was a lovely sixty-room building which sat on several acres of land with the most beautiful lake.

Croydon was close enough to Town to ensure those who had been invited would have made the journey. And Christopher had prevailed upon his friend to invite the baroness and her delightful daughter.

Everyone was gathered on the south side lawns for archery, and competition had been underway. Miss Cavanaugh had brightened upon seeing him and had bestowed in his direction a very improper and dazzling smile. Everyone had noted it.

Delighted with her genuineness he had bowed and charmingly greeted her, even if he had been more circumspect in his admiration. While he had burned to compliment her beauty, he had instead discreetly admired her prettiness. She was clad in a lime green cinched waist gown with a close-fitting bodice trimmed with white lace, which accentuated her lovely and curvaceous frame. Miss Cavanaugh's dark hair was caught in a simple chignon with a matching green hat perched jauntily atop her head, curling tendrils dangled kissing her rosy cheeks.

Bancroft had craftily paired Miss Cavanaugh with him, after noting Christopher's interest. Her mother seemed delighted by this, but the lady appeared a bit puzzled by his attention.

It soon became clear to him how very different she was from the other ladies present. How competitive. The other ladies used the opportunity of holding their bow to show off their trim figure and played with little seriousness. Not Miss Cavanaugh, her concentration to the game and her determination to win was remarked upon, and not favorably. It seemed everyone was of a mind to think she should let him win.

Thwack! Her arrow hit the target which sat a remarkable one hundred yards dead center.

A hush fell over the gathering, and admiration rushed through him.

The baroness appeared unduly anxious, and it occurred to him she also believed her daughter should allow him to win.

She strolled toward the target and acting with the impulse he fell in to step beside her.

"Do you not know dukes should always win," he murmured.

She shot him a side eye glance and then back at the small gathering, which avidly watched their interactions.

"Do you want me to allow you to win, Your Grace?"

"Would you?"

She grinned, and the prettiness of it made his heart lurch.

"No. but it is evident everyone expects me to allow you to win."

"And you take delight in denying their expectations."

She laughed and then fell silent for a minute. They reached the target, and she plucked the arrow from its center and handed it to him.

"Your turn," she murmured, her eyes dancing with mirth.

With a smile, he nocked his bow and let loose his arrow. Of course, he was not as precise as Miss Cavanaugh, and with a sweet chortle his mother would no doubt think vulgar, she made it known she had won.

"I demand a rematch."

"On what grounds?"

"I was unfairly distracted."

A smile quivered at the corners of her mouth. "By what?"

"By you, Miss Cavanaugh. Your crooked endearing smile, your scent, the way you tuck your hair behind your ear, and the unfettered way in which you laugh."

Her face flushed a delicate, rosy hue, and her eyes lit with amusement and something soft. He wanted to explore that softness more than he wanted his next breath.

"Do not blame the weakness of your play on my crooked smile." Then she headed back toward their party, as if afraid of how intimate their conversation had grown. He hurried to fall in step with her.

"Does my frankness make you uncomfortable," he asked gently.

"No." She turned her head, looking up into his face with pleading eyes. "It makes me hunger, and it is that reaction which I find alarming."

His mouth went dry at the echo of need in her voice. *Thank God it is mutual.*

They continued in silence until they reached their small party. Archery continued for another hour or so, before everyone retired for a lavish luncheon. A couple of hours later, several blankets were laid out on the lawns, and many guests reposed upon them playing cribbage.

Miss Cavanaugh had teasingly engaged him with their game of chess, and now they strolled together under the watchful eyes of her mother and what felt like society, but in truth was only about two dozen guests.

However, the guests soon noted he was extremely particular in his attention to Miss Cavanaugh, and their questioning stares were now becoming quite evident. When she realized it, she faltered into astonishing stillness and peered up at him.

"Your Grace..."

"Miss Cavanaugh," he replied with tender amusement.

She directed him a look of bemused inquiry. He was heartened to see no animosity or judgment, but a distinct hint of curiosity and desire. The memory of their kiss lingered in her eyes along with the sometimes soft, and hesitant manner in which she tried to stare discreetly. "You are spending an inordinate amount of time with me today." *As if we are courting* hung unspoken in the air. A frightening and thrilling question in equal measure.

"I find your company to be most charming."

Her eyes widened. "Certainly not more than any other lady here. Miss Charlotte Hufford has been sending us very unpleasant glances. At first, I thought it was because I trounced her in archery, but I am beginning to suspect it is entirely something else!"

He placed a hand across his chest. "Perhaps my hopes to kiss you is not as masked as I'd intended."

She blushed rosily, the pulse at her throat fluttering madly, and stammered, "Yo...you should not say such wicked things."

"I cannot help wanting to woo you."

The woman laughed. "How excessively diverting." And he could see that she did not believe him to be sincere.

While past hurts had not made her bitter and wretched, she was untrusting. And it made Christopher question the tender yearning he saw in her lovely gaze.

"Do you still wish to exact revenge on me, Miss Cavanaugh?"

Pippa's eyes swiftly raised and held an arrested expression. "I declare I never stopped."

This piece of audacity was uttered in the most casual, and indifferent manner.

Amusement and devilry stirred. "If you are determined to unmask me as a debaucher, I daresay I should provide you with some material."

"My attention is snared," she said, her eyes laughing at him.

"The very first image you looked at...I want to do that to *you*...here, now. I wonder, Miss Cavanaugh; will you be wicked with me?"

He felt briefly surprised by himself for he had never been the one to cross sensual wits with a lady of society.

Though they did not touch, raw need flamed in her eyes and burned him. Their gaze held, and in the depth of her eyes he saw the same compelling desire which he held for her, an all-consuming hunger and a need, but he also saw mistrust. Shadows were still in her eyes and a hint of fear.

He breathed evenly, controlling his body's startling reaction to well...her response. It *was* wicked, unexpected, proper, and so damn honest.

She glanced away breaking that contact, and he drew in a harsh breath at the loss of it. And without answering him, she walked away from him, every line in her body still in evident denial of the cravings stirring in her heart and body for him.

Her mother appeared shocked at her daughter's abrupt actions, and made apologies then bid him a good day as she hurried after Miss Cavanaugh.

CHAPTER 11

A soft rain pattered against the windows of the countess's drawing room. The slight rain had been unexpected and had halted the walk into town Pippa had promised Miranda who wanted to order hats and laces. The plan had been to visit a tea shop afterward for refreshment, or Gunter's for an ice. Instead of the outing, they were ensconced in the drawing room, a merry fire crackling in the hearth. Pippa was reading the serial *Oliver Twist* by Charles Dickens, which was the current rage and quite deserving of its popularity. The writing was evocative and painted a very vivid picture of the injustices of England, yet Pippa's attention was torn from the riveting words. She did not believe in such nonsense like magic, but if someone offered a potion with the promise it would allow her to stop thinking of a certain duke, she would consume it within a blink.

It had been a week since the outing to Croydon

where she had fled from the temptation of the duke. He had flirted, he had teased, and she hadn't known how to handle it, so she had run from the beautiful temptation of it all. She liked him far too much. In his gaze there had been a simmering heat, a promise of wicked lusts, and everything inside of her had craved to respond.

I cannot help wanting to woo you.

She drew in a hard, deep breath. Such ridiculous nonsense, and very similar to words Mr. Nigel Williamsfield had said to Pippa on so many occasions with earnest adoration and flattery. Except, the duke hadn't been artful. She'd only sensed raw honesty. *Also, I would be foolish to believe*, and Pippa accepted she must be a damn fool, for she felt the duke wanted her. Every stare had communicated his desire and admiration. Her heart begged her logical mind to take the duke's hand and go on the adventure he invited. Even if only once.

Miranda lowered the fashion magazine she had been reading. "I am terribly excited about tonight's masquerade ball. Lord Aaron has been paying me the loveliest compliments, and I daresay I find him quite charming," she said with a tinkling laugh.

Pippa frowned. "Lord Aaron? I thought he had a tendre for Miss Elisabeth Fairfax." At least that is what she had written some weeks ago as Lady W, and the couple's popularity within the ton had soared, and everyone had celebrated the match.

Miranda arched an elegant brow. "Everyone

thought the earl would have offered for Miss Fairfax because of her dowry. It is rumored to be one hundred thousand pounds and a villa in the south side of France. Why everyone knows that is the only reason she had so many *beaux* this season. She is rather plain faced and coarse in her manners."

"I think her charming and quite elegant in her manners," Pippa rebutted. Not at all pleased with Miranda's disparaging words.

Miranda sniffed. "You are far too careless in your compliments, but that is expected with the company you've been keeping."

They stared at each other across the expanse of the drawing room. "And what company is that?" Pippa said softly.

"Carlyle!" Miranda snapped, her eyes flashing with a good deal of ire.

Hearing the name startled Pippa, for this was the first time in weeks Miranda spoke of the duke. After Pippa had seen his genuine shock at her accusation of his debauchery, and his earnest offer to call upon her mother after kissing her, she had attempted to speak of him to Miranda to clarify what had happened between the two. But Miranda had declined to have any discourse about the man.

"I've warned you of his odious—"

"The duke did not seduce you," Pippa whispered, gently closing *Oliver Twist*.

With a gasp, Miranda surged to her feet. "Why

ever would you say this now," she said, her eyes darting to the closed door of the drawing room.

"The countess and mamma have gone for an early morning ride in the park, and I am certain they have sought shelter from the rain. We shan't be disturbed."

Miranda huffed. "I do not wish to speak of it. That is the past, and I do not wish to recall the humiliation of it all."

Pippa considered her friend and everything she had been learning of the duke. He was undoubtedly wicked in the manner he had stolen kisses, more than kisses, for he had compromised her heart. If Pippa was honest, most days she wanted to fall at the altar of his debauchery, and she could not blame him for her weakness in wanting his sensual adventures. However, he hadn't made any false promises, nor had he attempted to force her or even seduce her.

Why then would he have tried to seduce Miranda? She was not worldly, and far too innocent for the duke. "I despised the duke because of what he did to you. I've spoken to him...on a few occasions..."

"Then the rumors are true?"

"I am not sure what the gossips are saying." Pippa had ignored reading tattles except the ones she contributed. "I am saying, I have formed my own idea of the duke, and it does not match with your account," she said gently.

A flush rose in Miranda's cheek. "And what is your opinion?"

Pippa braced herself. "He does not seem to be the

sort of man who would behave with such rank dishonor. I've seen a great kindness and consideration of others in him."

Miranda's lips curved in a sneer. "You are hardly the best judge of a man's character. If you had been, surely you would have been more discerning of Nigel!"

Pippa gasped, and regret lined Miranda's face.

"Oh Pippa, I am ghastly. Forgive me." She took a deep breath. "It is always difficult to think of the duke...to speak of him."

"You must tell me what happened, for I have promised you not to tell a soul so to ask Christopher for the details is not something I can do, but I must know the truth."

Miranda froze, her eyes flashing with indecipherable emotions. "The duke is *Christopher* to *you?*"

Jealousy and hurt were thick in her tone, and Pippa flinched and closed her eyes. She now felt like a cad. The memories of his touch and heated kisses filled her. She shouldn't have allowed him, no matter how compelling she'd found him. Not when Miranda's heart was still hopelessly entangled with the duke. Oh, how wretched Pippa felt. "That was a mistake, I—"

"Do you love him?" Miranda demanded, fisting her hands at her side.

"What? Of course not! Do not be so absurd." The denial made her heart tremble. *Dear God*. Was she falling in love with the duke? How preposterous would that be?

Miranda folded her arms under her bosom, impatient annoyance evident in the elegant line of her posture. "Then why do you need to know more?"

Because the honor Pippa had spied several times of his character had undermined Miranda's claim in Pippa's opinion. "I should be astonished if I discovered that the duke did seduce you, Miranda, please be honest with me."

"I never said he seduced me," she cried.

Pippa stared at her friend, not wanting to accept the logical conclusion. "You tried to compromise him," she guessed faintly. "*Deliberately*...and he refused you. Oh Miranda, what were you thinking to act with such rank disregard of your reputation and standing in society?"

Fat tears rolled down her cheeks. "I wanted to be his duchess," she said on a shaky breath. She sank onto the sofa, burying her face in her hands, her slender form convulsed by deep sobs.

"He did not deserve the discredit you laid at his door." And she owed him an apology, as Pippa Cavanaugh and Lady W. She closed her eyes, already envisioning the fight from Mr. Bell. He would not want to print a retraction only more salubrious speculation. Pippa felt wretched. "If you knew the manner of man the duke is, you would not have acted so silly." No wonder Miranda had not wanted to inform the Earl and Countess.

"And you do?" Miranda said with scathing contempt.

"I do not wish to fight with you, but you let me believe the worst of the duke when you had been at fault, Miranda."

Her eyes flashed with ire. "He did see me naked!"

Pippa stood and walked over to her. "Did he kiss you? Did he seduce you with words and touches, taking off your clothes or assisting you to take them off?"

Miranda blushed and turned away. "No!"

Pippa continued, "And did he invite you to his room?"

Her shoulder trembled. "No. We sat beside each other at dinner, and he was so charming and attentive. We spoke of the weather, his travels to India, tigers, and elephants. I thought...mamma was so certain he was interested. She praised me for snaring his regard when so many others had failed. Then I heard him speaking of possibly traveling to Europe for several months, and I recalled the rumors of the Russian heiress. I...I had to act."

Pippa felt such disappointment in her friend's conduct...and in her own gullibility she almost cried. How ready she had been to cast the duke in the same dishonorable light as Nigel and her father when he had not deserved it. "You went into his room," Pippa said softly, knowing Miranda's nature of pursuing what she wanted at all cost.

"I waited in my robe, and when he entered, I shrugged it from my shoulders."

Pippa's heart beat a furious rhythm as she asked, "And what did he do?"

"Turned away!" Miranda said on a pained wail. "He simply turned away and said nothing would induce him to marry a calculating wench, not even the threat of a scandal, and left his room. I was so mortified."

Now she understood the surprise in his eyes when she had refused his visit to her mother because of his kiss. How many ladies had tried to compromise him? How many had only seen the title and wealth and not the man beneath all of that? "You were ill-judged to act so, Miranda!"

"I was not!"

Pippa recognized an exercise in futility when she saw one. Miranda would not take responsibility. "I am disappointed that you will not see it. The duke deserves an apology from both of us. It would be poor of your character if you did not render him one."

Then she walked from the room, ignoring her softly sobbing friend.

In the hallway, she spied her mother hurrying toward the drawing room with a letter in her hand. There was a sheen of distress in her mother's eyes.

Pippa increased her pace. "Mamma? Is all well?"

"A letter..." she took a deep breath. "A letter came

from *her*." Her mother handed over a peach vellum sheet of paper.

Pippa took it, feeling astonished to see it addressed from Miss Annmarie Calvert, of a New York address. Pippa guided her mother toward a smaller sitting room for privacy. It upset Pippa to see her mother so clearly rattled by the other woman's letter. She slit it open delicately with a letter opener.

Dear Miss Pippa Cavanaugh,

It is with regret that I write to you, your father, Lord Cavanaugh has taken ill. Doctors attend him and have given good reports, and I have hope he will recover. It is not at all certain, and he has begged for his wife and daughter to visit him in New York. I suspect your love for him is low, but I beseech you, Miss Cavanaugh, to attend to his bedside. I've enclosed a draft for one thousand pounds—

Unable to carry on reading, she lowered the letter and handed it to her mother. It seemed today was the day for dreadful revelations. Her heart pounded, and her throat was tight with pain and worry. How Pippa loathed that she worried about a man who had turned his back on his family with little regard for the circumstances in which he had left them! And now to demand they drop everything and voyage on a ship, so that he might soothe his conscience?

Oh, papa, you wretched lout! She swiped at the tear that rolled down her cheek. *Please do not die.* The idea of losing him in such a permanent manner felt unbearable.

"I will not go," her mother said, her voice rough

with pain. "How dare she ask it of me? How dare he ask for me…after…after what he has done. I do not care that he is in a sick bed!"

The memories swirled between them, of watching her father pack his various valises, precious books, and journals from the library, and even a few paintings from the ancestral gallery. It had felt so frightening and permanent. Pippa had sat on the top of the staircase watching as her mother abandoned her dignity as she'd rushed behind him crying and demanding to know what he was doing. Pippa would always recall the petite brunette who had sat in a parked carriage and waited as a husband and father left his family without explanations.

"I do not know if I should go," she said softly. "What if he should die…what if papa dies?"

Her mother straightened her shoulders. "You should go to him."

"Mamma?"

"I can see that you want to, and I shall not resent you for it. He's your father. He loves…loved and cared for you for fifteen years. The pain of his leaving cannot replace all those wonderful memories." Her mother took a bracing breath and continued, "It is cruel of me to say this, but if your father dies, I will be free to marry the man I am falling in love with."

Pippa's hand flew to her throat, and she stared at her mother.

"You…you love the viscount?" she demanded, wholly taken aback.

"I do," mamma said quietly. "I believe I do and I am not afraid of such sentiments again. We are very discreet for I would never forgive myself if...if I hurt your chances with the Duke of Carlyle."

Pippa could not help smiling, but she said very earnestly, "Mamma, I have no chance with a duke! A man such as Carlyle will marry only for power and connections. I would be silly to lead my heart to hope beyond my expectations. You worry for naught, I assure you. But I will always urge you to be careful with your heart."

Her mother's lips set in a stubborn line. "The duke has taken a marked fancy to you, and even the scandal sheets have made mention of it. Our invitations have soared, and not because of my dear friend's patronage. It is because of the attention the duke has shown you. Today flowers were delivered here for you. Several bouquets of roses, and lilies."

Pippa had seen them, but flowers delivered courtesy of gentleman callers were commonplace at the countess's townhouse. "I...thought they were for Miranda."

"No," her mother said triumphantly. "They were *all* for you, from gentlemen who had hardly taken any notice before. The duke paying attention to you goes a far way to restoring your reputation. There is a reason for the duke's interest, and we must not discount it."

"Perhaps he wishes me to occupy another

position in his life. Like Harriette Wilson for the Duke of Wellington."

"Pippa!" her mother cried eyes wide with distress. "That is the ghastliest thing to suggest. You are a young lady of good standing and...and..."

"Forgive me, mamma. I did not mean to upset you." She stood, made her way over, and pressed a kiss to her cheek. "I am overwrought by the news of papa. However, it is no excuse; I should have minded my tongue and been more ladylike in my thoughts."

Her mother nodded graciously, and after a few more minutes of discussing the situation of her papa, Pippa excused herself and retreated to her room. Still, Pippa devoted the better part of the afternoon to the composition of a letter to Miss Calvert after reading the entire letter. Pippa informed her father's mistress she would visit New York post haste, but Lady Cavanaugh would not be traveling with her. Miss Calvert had already planned for passage, and Pippa was to depart for New York aboard *Maiden Anne* in two weeks.

There was a return ticket dated almost two months from today. The lady's action was audacious to assume the length of visit Pippa would be able to commit to. But she did not quibble, for once she saw her father, she would book a return passage immediately. Or perhaps she would stay till the pre-booked date and learn about her siblings.

A pang tore through her heart. She had a brother of five years, a sister of two years. And Miss Calvert was now with child. Three siblings that would have no connection with her mother but who would always be a part of Pippa's family. What could she possibly say to them? She could not imagine what she would feel upon seeing her father again. Sorrow? Joy? Relief? Anger? Unable to bear thinking of it all anymore, she crawled into her bed, closed her eyes, and let all the uncertainty drift away with the oblivion of sleep.

CHAPTER 12

A few hours later, Pippa sat before her vanity, disinterested in the masquerade ball which had been heralded by the newspapers as the event of the season. She had daringly decided to dress like a gentleman of leisure and had propositioned Miss Tilby to attain the clothing. Pippa was now garbed in dark trousers which fitted her rounded bottom too well. Knee-high boots encased her calves, she wore a matching dark jacket, a snowy white undershirt, a cravat that had been painful to tie, and a wine-red waistcoat. And she'd topped off her ensemble with a short dark wig and a dark mask which covered her eyes and face. The final touches were the beaver hat perched rakishly atop her head and an ebony cane.

The idea had seemed naughty and adventurous when she'd first conceived it, only now, Pippa did not think she appeared like a boy at all. Her curves were too richly pronounced, her breasts evident beneath the waistcoat. Nor was she thrilled to mingle with the crowd, listening and noting the latest scandals to excite society as Lady W.

She had decided to leave for New York, and in two weeks, she would set sail away from whatever was burgeoning between her and the duke. There it was again, that unfathomable ache whenever she thought of leaving and never understanding all that she felt for Christopher. Though she had decided on a course of action, Pippa's nerves would not settle. Following the impulses that were beating in her heart for the last hour, she departed the countess's townhouse, and daringly strode through the rapidly darkening streets until she saw a hackney to hail.

Her guise as a young man was successful, for no one accosted her or glanced at her oddly. The journey from Russel Square to Grosvenor street was a blessedly short one. Evidently, her nerves would have deserted her if she had traveled any longer. She felt breathless and uncomfortably hot. Upon exiting the hackney, she took the familiar path through the side gates and made her way around the gardens to the window leading to the library.

Sense and propriety would not convince her to turn away and attend the masquerade ball only a few houses away. Pippa tested the window and smiled to see that it was unlatched. Had he been expecting her? Though she'd been prepared to use her trade tricks once again. She hauled herself up and slipped into the duke's library. Pippa realized immediately he had anticipated her presence. The chess board rested on the lush blue and silver Aubusson carpet in the center of the room, and all the sofas had been pushed out of the way, creating ample space for them. Several cushions littered the carpet in wild disarray. It was clear he intended for them to play there, sprawled on the rug and pillows. How indecent and quite lovely!

A smile tugged at her lips. The low table was the only furniture near their play area, and it held several crystal decanters of liquor. Different types since their colors ranged from amber, red, and dark brown. Her gaze scanned the room, searching for the duke. When she found him, Pippa pressed her hand to her chest, wondering at the fast yet delicate way it pounded. The duke lay on the carpet near the merrily crackling fire, several cushions behind his head and shoulders, and atop the man was about five wolfhound puppies. Pippa could not credit her eyes. Stranger still, the duke seemed to be sleeping. A few of the puppies slumbered, and two danced over the muscles of his chest, nipping at his chin and licking his face.

Pippa giggled when he grabbed one of the puppies and bit him back. The puppy took that as a sign for more vigorous romping and tail wagging. She had never seen such a sight! The duke's eyes snapped open at her low laugh, and upon seeing her, a smile curved his lips—one of sin and decadence.

"Walking on the wild side, are we?"

Something wicked, heated, and undefinable

stirred inside her then. She stumbled back, almost scared at the intensity of feelings.

Love...is this love? This need to fling myself in his arms and kiss him without reservations, to lay atop him as the puppies did? To tell him of my day and ask him about his?

He pushed the puppies off him and settled them one by one in the center of a few cushions. The care he touched them with indicated a deep love. He scratched one of the puppy's belly, and it flattened its ears and lolled its tongue out gratefully. The duke laughed—the rich, low sound striking her heart with a weakening blow, and at that moment, Pippa fell in love with Christopher Worth, the Duke of Carlyle. A sensation she had never felt before wrapped itself around her heart, before invading it with pure warmth and happiness.

Acting on impulse, she went over, knelt, and scooped up the furry little creature, hugging it close to her. "I've never had a pet before! How adorable they are." The pup wriggled from her arm, and with a delighted laugh, she let it go.

The duke stood and held out his hand, assisting her up.

"I'm leaving for New York," she blurted, unable to understand why that was the first thing she said.

The duke had faltered into stillness, a denial flashing in the piercing silver of his eyes. "When?" he asked softly.

They stood too close, and she took several steps

toward the window she'd climbed through. "Fourteen days."

He considered this before asking, "And will you return?"

"Yes...but I do not know when. Perhaps a month or more."

They stared at each other in the silence that settled in the library. He took a deep breath, and to her mind, there was a hint of forlornness in the sound.

Why did she feel so horribly vulnerable? "Did you..." she spread her arms wide to encompass the room. "Did you know I would come?"

"I hoped. My library has been in this state for days," he said gruffly. "Do not leave. I must wash my hands." He gathered the wriggling puppies, and then with clipped strides, he exited the room closing the door behind him softly.

Oh, what am I doing? She had hurtled herself impetuously to his home, and now she was confounded as to why she was truly present. Pippa turned toward the window, but her retreat was halted by the return of the duke. This time when the door closed there was a distinct *snick*. "I'm not sure why I am here," she said.

"To play chess of course."

She looked helplessly at him. Then Pippa removed the beaver hat and rested it on the desk with her cane.

"The wig too, I want to see your glorious hair."

He shot a challenging look at her, which she met with a faint smile. But she slowly removed the wig, resting it with her other things. Appreciative warmth lit in his eyes, and she held herself still while he came over to her. He touched her cheek with the tips of his fingers, and for a moment, she savored the wonderful caress. How was it possible to reach the age of two and twenty and never felt such delight from simply touching another?

"You are very beautiful, Pippa."

She deeply breathed in the warm, scented breeze that wafted gently in through the window behind her, hoping to settle her composure.

"Come now, my admiration and sentiments cannot be unknown to you."

"And what sentiments are those?" she asked bravely.

He stepped back, giving her breathing space she hadn't realized she needed.

There was a good deal of amusement in his eyes as they rested on her face. "I like you," he said. "Now let's play chess."

She tried to speak but dared not trust her voice. Instead, she lowered herself onto the carpet before the chess board. He sat opposite her and poured drinks into two glasses. She took the one he offered. "Whisky again?"

He smiled. "Bourbon."

She took a tentative sip. A sweet aromatic flavor washed over her tongue, but she could not name the taste, and she was unsure if she liked it. "Are you not appalled by my unladylike qualities?"

"The opposite," he said warmly. "Your adventurous nature is quite appealing. I find prim and proper tedious at times."

Biting back a smile, she leaned forward and assessed the chess board. "You put in our moves." All the ones they had done mentally and jokingly had been inserted by the duke.

"Of course." He leaned forward as well, watching the board, and she was conscious of the intimate closeness of their heads.

"I am happy you are here, and not at Lady Appleton's masquerade ball," she said softly.

Pippa felt the touch of his eyes against her skin, but she did not take her eyes away from the chess pieces.

"I'm glad you came. Though I wonder what prompted you."

"I was scared, and somehow when I am with you.... I just knew I would not feel scared anymore." The words were out before she could prevent them.

A finger nudged under her chin. The slightest pressure was exerted as he lifted her face to his. "What scared you?"

There was a watchful, ruthless air about him, and suddenly Pippa knew he would not take kindly to anything that threatened her. The knowledge wrapped around her, filling her with indescribable emotions. "It scared me that I may love my father still," she admitted, the ache in her heart growing wider.

Christopher pushed a wisp of hair behind her ear and then lowered his arm. "And that is terrible?"

She felt bereft of his touch and wanted to lean into him but mastered the desire. Pippa picked up a piece and toyed with it, the game forgotten, as the need to share her doubts and agonies overwhelmed everything else. "What kind of person am I to love someone who has hurt my mother and me so horribly. How can I still care for him? How can I be so weak?"

Pippa took several sips of her bourbon.

"It takes courage to love someone who has hurt you before. The weakness would be bitterness and a cold, unforgiving heart. It is easier to be angry. It takes an unfathomable character to love and forgive. Do not think you are weak for still loving your father, Pippa. Never that. I only see a strength to be admired."

The honesty in his gaze pierced Pippa deeply. "That is how you see me?"

"Yes."

"Thank you," she whispered, desperately wanting to hug him, kiss him even.

"You have my only bishop. Please put him back," he said with light humor. "I believe before you go home, Miss Cavanaugh, we should discuss matters of the heart. Wouldn't you agree?"

With a smile she said, "My heart has an annoying tendency to act wayward"—she leaned over to make a very deliberate move, hoping to entice him into moving his king— "and is easily deceived. Not sure there is much to discuss there."

"Ah, mine has always been still." He considered her with an almost bemused frown. "Until *you*. Now it beats. Now it wonders. Now it aches. And that is all because of you, Miss Cavanaugh."

They were so hopelessly ineligible that it had never dawned in her mind that he would ever think to consider her with sweetly intimate wonder. What did she have to offer him other than her wit and humor? Perhaps he jested or offered empty flattery, but there had been a note of sincerity in his voice, and his smile was a tender caress against her senses. Pippa's heart ached with wants and needs she had long suppressed. "We would not suit," she said chidingly, taking another sip of her bourbon. *I want you so*, her mind and heart cried.

"You possess qualities I admire most ardently— kindness, loyalty, and simmering wickedness. You meant to bring me down because of your love for a friend. *Me*...the Duke of Carlyle. Laughable indeed but admirable."

The mock outrage in his expression pulled a light laugh from Pippa. "How freeing life is for a duke...or is it so for all gentlemen?"

He tipped his drink to his head and finished in one long swallow, before resting his glass on the rug. "The denial of self is very painful."

"You speak from experience I suppose," she said archly.

"Has there been anything you've wanted to do that was improper?"

Everything I do with you.

He must have seen the answer in her eyes for he continued with, "It feels terrible, does it not, to refuse your heart what it hungers for? Most often this denial is because of other people's expectations."

"My presence here easily establishes my impropriety," she said repressively. "Yet everyone says you are so *very* proper...the Duke of Saints."

Pleasure lit in his eyes. "Ah, Miss Cavanaugh, surely you know my wicked heart by now?"

Incorrigible! When she made no reply, he leaned in closer.

"What's going on in that beautiful mind?" he mused.

"The heart can be deceiving," she said softly, hinting at the fears and uncertainty of falling too deeply into him. Because she wanted him more than she cared to admit.

Knowledge burned in his gaze, and she recalled he had been a witness to the humiliation and hurt rendered by Mr. Nigel Williamsfield.

"I've been waiting for you, Pippa," Christopher said with all sobriety, and his silver gaze steady on hers. "I've been waiting for you."

CHAPTER 13

So many sensations tumbled through Pippa, she felt her heart was breaking with the intensity. As if the duke sensed she had no words, he pressed a kiss to her forehead, and her breath hitched. His mouth drifted along her cheek, and she wanted to rub against him like a cat.

"Tell me," he murmured. "Have you ever felt like this?"

She swallowed. "Like what?"

"I ache for your kiss," he said, perilously close to her mouth. "The feel and taste of it was a bright, beautiful heat, like the sun on my face." A soft press against the corner of her mouth. "I want to devour your lips, and suck that pretty little tongue into my mouth."

She nearly lost her breath at the look of wicked sensuality on his face. Pippa had dreamed of this, ached for him, and now she would live in the moment. With a groan of denial, she pulled away, surged to her feet and started pacing.

The duke stood, watching her with his unfathomable gaze.

"I want you," she gasped.

His eyes closed and the flat of his palm pressed against his heart as if he was profoundly relieved. Christopher's gaze snapped open, and she stared into a storm of needs and want. Within a few strides, he was before her.

"This...this is reckless!" she breathed. Without waiting for his answer, Pippa went on her tiptoes, fell against his chest, and gripped his neck with one hand pulling him to her. "I want you to do every wicked thing I've seen in your drawings."

Dear God. For a second, the hunger and the lust that fired in his eyes stole her sanity. She felt lightheaded, off balance. His breathing was harsh and heavy in the still air of the library as his forehead pressed against hers.

"Are you certain?" he demanded gruffly, still the gentleman.

"I know this will be a mistake," she whispered on a sigh, kissing the bridge of his nose. "I know it, but I cannot halt the cravings in my heart." Trembling and scarcely able to breathe, she touched her lips to his.

"No...this is fate...destiny." It was his turn to place a kiss atop her nose.

Pippa was seduced, for she had caved to the reckless impulses beating in her soul for this man.

Perhaps it was the two glasses of bourbon she had consumed for the night. She closed her eyes briefly, before opening them to peer into the honest hunger within his silver gaze. *I'm not a coward, it's not the bourbon*. It was the man himself and the fear she would never experience anything as beautiful, glorious, and exciting as this night with him.

"I want all your kisses," she breathed huskily.

He stiffened, a flush working along his cheekbones. "And I want to give them to you, but—"

She caught his mouth with hers, shocking herself and him it seemed for he had faltered into stillness. Then his mouth moved above hers, coaxing and seducing in equal measure. A whimper of pleasure passed from her mouth to his, and with a sigh, her lips parted and allowed him entry.

Fire. This delight was a fire she wanted to consume her world. Rioting sensations arched through her, and she shivered into his arms. They broke apart, and he shrugged from his jacket, shirt, waistcoat and placed it on the soft carpet. He had a wide chest, tapered down to a lean waist. Broad shoulders and sculpted muscles went with it. He was so beautiful!

Christopher prowled over to her and tugged at the loosely tied cravat and slid it from her neck.

"We'll be using this before the night is out," he murmured with wicked sensuality.

Desire made her feel weak, and her fingers trembled as she attempted to take off her jacket. His touch halted her, and he took evident pleasure in removing the jacket, waistcoat, and shirt she wore.

Pippa did not know where she got the courage to stand before the duke, naked from the waist up. But the worship in his eyes as he beheld her, suppressed all anxiety she felt. His hands skimmed her breasts, and the jolt of heat that tore through her made her gasp breathily.

"You are ravishing," he said with carnal reverence before kneeling, lifting her feet one by one and removing her boots.

"Stockings beneath your trousers, Miss Cavanaugh? How inventive."

Then he peeled off the trousers, leaving her in said stockings alone. He slowly peered up at the length of her from his crouch. Her entire body blushed red, but she held herself still under his devouring gaze. She felt his eyes, like a physical touch, on every dip and curve of her body. She didn't know what to expect, only that she craved his attention.

Christopher stood and tugged her into his arms. The night closed around them, holding their passion and secrets close. They came together, kissing even more passionately than before, and she could only clasp his shoulders and surrendered to his ravishment as he bore her down to the cushions and pillows on the carpeted floor.

"Pippa," he groaned against her lips as if tortured.

"I want you...and tonight I will be wicked." This

was her choice. It was unlikely he or anyone would marry her, and that was fine, for Pippa knew enough of independence to believe she could forge a future for herself and flourish. Tonight she would choose a moment to remember for her entire life, memories of pleasure and not those of hurt and disappointment. And she would do it with a man she was falling irrevocably in love with.

"I do not want the risk of falling with a child...do you know how to prevent this?" she tried to sound worldly, but the blush that covered her entire body pulled a tender smile to his lips.

"I do." Another kiss of violent tenderness before their lips parted. "I want to court you...do this properly..."

Her heart lurched inside, and she searched his gaze, unable to trust in this declaration. It was the passion, the lust speaking. She was the daughter of a disgraced baron, and he the duke of eminent power and respectability. The entire *ton* knew the kind of lady he was expected to marry, and it was not her. The false promises Mr. Nigel Williamsfield had made suddenly reared their head. "I have no expectations of you," she said with frankness. Yet her heart screamed for more.

This was proving more dangerous than she'd anticipated.

Christopher pressed a kiss to the corner of her lips, and down to her neck. "Trust me," he murmured along her jaw. "I would not ever willingly hurt you."

She wanted to believe in his words so much her throat ached. "Why not?"

He cupped her cheeks, tipping her face up toward his. "Because you are already precious."

Then he took her lips with carnal tenderness. Her body felt flushed and unfamiliar. A shiver of alarm and anticipation in equal measure worked through Pippa when he dragged his fingers along her stocking-clad shin.

He trailed his fingers up the length of her leg, and over her silken stockings. Then he explored farther, letting his hand drift up the sensitive skin of her inner thigh to the wet heart of her.

"Oh!" she gasped at the delightful intimacy and then moaned when he parted her folds with one of his fingers.

Their gaze collided and she could not remove her eyes from his. All her senses became centered around the feather-light pressure against her sex. Then he slipped a finger into her, and she arched sharply off the ground.

"I've got you," he murmured, taking her lips with soft, soothing kisses.

Each stroke into her wet, stretched sex was a shock of exquisite pleasure, and Pippa whimpered craving more. The shivering sensation low in her stomach felt as if she were falling.

"How adventurous do you wish to be tonight?"

In answer, she leaned forward and put her lips against the naked flesh of his chest, parted her lips, and let her tongue swipe across his nipple. He groaned, and she almost purred. She peppered kisses up to his throat and chin. Pippa was unable to voice the wanton leanings in her heart. But then...she'd never been a coward. "I want endless kisses," she murmured against his mouth, before kissing him deeply.

His mouth moved more urgently against hers in a kiss of exquisite tenderness, while his hands learned each dip and swell of her body. It was as if each place he touched caught fire and burned long after he had moved on. With nips in between kisses, he awoke the carnal creature within her. His hand glided over her breast, the lightest of touches, then his tongue curled around her nipple.

Pippa moaned weakly.

"How beautiful you are," he murmured roughly. "I want to woo you...court you. I am falling into your smiles, your cleverness, your impropriety, and I do not want to stop, Miss Cavanaugh. I do not ever want to stop."

She found it impossible to understand what he hoped to gain by his extraordinary declaration. "Woo me?"

A kiss was pressed against her lips. "Woo you... marry you."

She did laugh then, startling them both. Pippa sobered, staring at him, not trusting the sweet feeling bursting in her heart. *Oh, Christopher*. His name whispered in her mind like a caress. A sweet, piquant longing struck her in the stomach, thick and undeniable. *Dear God.* She hesitated, in equal surprise and doubt. "You jest with my hopes and emotions."

"No jesting," he murmured. "You make me feel, Pippa, a thousand sensations, hope, and dreams, and I can tell I am eager to experience a million more with you."

He had a look in his eyes that touched something cold way down inside of her and thawed it.

"I do not believe in sacrificing my happiness to suit my family's notions of respectability," he murmured, kissing her lips with such tenderness a lump rose in her throat. "You are not disreputable. You are kind and wonderful, improper and wanton, and I adore everything about you."

"But we hardly know each other," she said searching the face above hers, wondering if he could really feel the same desperate want she endured.

"Oh? Many people in society simply marry after a few weeks of walking in the park and dancing at a ball a few times. Or they marry because of wealth and connections. We've had much more than many alliances in society, and I daresay you like and want me as much as I do you."

"Heaven help me, but I do, Christopher!" She fused her lips with his, kissing him with all the building passion in her heart.

Heat raced from where his lips kissed along her cheek, down her nape and shoulder before moving slowly, with shudder-inducing sensations, down her spine. He shifted her slightly, so she lay on her stomach. He kissed along the delicate length of her spine, the curve of her buttocks.

"You have the lushest backside I've ever had the pleasure to see," he murmured, biting down on the globes of her flesh. Pippa moaned arching up.

He caressed her hips in a long, soothing stroke, then peeled off the stockings until she was completely naked. He turned her around and spread her legs wide. Mortification and sensuality blushed through her body, and she stared at him helplessly. Christopher rose and removed the rest of his clothing until he was just as naked as Pippa.

"You are the beautiful one," she said softly, amazed by the corded strength of his body, the chiseled elegance of each defined muscle. And that part of him was nothing like the pictures in that book she and Miranda had found. The duke was much longer, and thicker.

She felt intoxicated on the sheer wicked excitement of being with him like this.

He knelt between her thighs, and his lips curved in a dangerous smile. Her heart thundered, and anticipation crested through her like a wave of fire. Her mind hazed in shock, and blistering desire when he lightly spanked her quim. The shock of it made her gasp even as the spike of heated lust had her arching her hips for more. Her heart began to race in heavy, erotic excitement as he spread her legs even wider.

"I knew you would be just as wicked," he praised, leaning over, and pressing an approving kiss above her navel.

Pippa panted, sweat slicking her skin, unbearable need and heat burning her from the inside. Her thighs fell wider apart at his urgings, and his broad shoulders wedged between them. Before Pippa could question his intention, he dipped his head and kissed her in a place she never dreamed could be kissed until she'd seen his erotic drawings.

"Christopher!" she cried out his name, her head falling back as her hips tilted forward, giving him access to her wet, aching sex. The feel of his tongue against her folds, licking and nibbling at her nub of pleasure was agony and ecstasy all rolled into one, and she didn't want it ever to end. She was awash in pleasure, and his name as it released from her lips was a scream of bliss. Every lick, every kiss, nibble, and touch felt like sin. She felt close, so close, to a pleasure she couldn't define.

His wicked, wicked lips latched onto her nub of pleasure, sucking mercilessly. Need as she'd never known before drew her taut, her hands fell into his thick hair and gripped, like something dark and wanton held her in an unrelenting grip. Sensation almost painful in its intensity peaked inside of Pippa. Her moan sounded raw and guttural as it gathered inside her like the most violent of storms, and she chased it, not afraid but hungering for the destruction she knew it would bring.

Unexpectedly it broke, and she shattered as ecstasy pulsed through her. The wailing, desperate cry that fell from her lips echoed in the library. While she was caught in the throes of unrelenting pleasure, he crawled over her, bracing himself on one elbow. His other hand slipped under her hips, arching her to him and with a surge of his hips, pushed his thick length in her wet, aching sex. The sharp pain was fleeting, but he held himself still, allowing her flesh to relax around his throbbing invasion.

He leaned down, brushing his lips against her forehead. "Marry me, Pippa," he whispered as his fingers rasped over the tender flesh of her stomach.

The stark lines of his face were heightened by desire and something tender. Almost like...love. "Yes," she said, despite the sudden pounding of doubt in her heart.

He held her wrists easily above her head, restraining her gently. Suddenly she could feel the phantom caress of a silken cravat and knew one day he would bind her, and she would surrender to all his wickedness.

Then he moved, withdrawing to thrust inside her with piercing deep strength. Pippa gasped, arching into the rough demands of his body. He released her hands, and she hugged him to her, clasping his shoulders and wrapping her legs high around his waist. He rode her, with raw passion, each driving stroke an exquisite burst of painful pleasure, each stroke edging Pippa toward the bright flames she could sense hovering.

Threads of reality dissolved beneath the lashing pleasure, and she clung to him, sobbing, with a desperate cry she surrendered to the sensation tearing through her body. And with a rough groan of deep satisfaction, he tumbled right along with her.

CHAPTER 14

Christopher kissed along Pippa's body, tickling the underside of her breasts with playful nips. She peered at him with shyness, her gaze dark and slumberous with the slow awakening of her sensuality. An enchanting ripple of laughter broke from her, and he closed his eyes, delighting in the sound.

Who would have thought that a laugh could so bewitch him?

"I must still go to New York," she said breathlessly. "My father is ill, and when I arrive, he may be recovered...or dead."

He kissed her shoulder soothingly. "I will come with you."

"That would be beyond improper!"

He came over her. "Not if we are man and wife. I'll procure a special license, and we'll marry before we depart."

The tentative hope in her eyes constricted his

breath. There were still shadows of doubt as if she believed his words were inconstant. He reposed against the pillows and tucked her into his side. With a sigh, he said, "I swear on my honor I did not seduce Lady Miranda."

"I know," she murmured, coasting a few of her fingers over his chest in an idle pattern.

"She told you?" he asked gruffly.

"I deduced the man I know could not be the one she described."

Pleasure burst inside his chest. "In truth, I cannot recall an encounter with her. She could have been the lady that tried to trap me in the conservatory at Lady Peckerham's ball, or the one who fainted in my arms at Lady Tunstall's Picnic, or the one who invaded my rooms at Lady Burrell's garden party. Many debutantes and even seasoned ladies have tried to compromise me into marriage."

"And you've deftly extricated yourself," she said with amusement. "I'm sorry you had to endure that. You deserve to be loved for the man you are, not your title."

Like I do, lingered in the air, and he wondered why she did not say the words he longed to hear. Was it that she was still uncertain? Might it be that she did not regard him with the same sentiments? Christopher scowled at the unusual press of uncertainty he felt.

"I must go before the dawn breaks."

He shifted, slipping her underneath him, and

cradling his weight between her thighs. A flush of want dusted her skin, accentuating the beauty of her large gray eyes, high, delicate cheekbones, and sweetly pouting lips. Anticipation built along with a craving that surpassed even the need to be in her body. He wanted her to trust him and to love him.

"Christopher?"

"Do you love me?"

She jolted and then stilled. Pippa stared at him for an impossibly long time. He realized he was holding his breath as he awaited her answer.

"I fear I do," she said softly, yet her voice still quivered with uncertainty.

"Let it not be a fear because you own my heart, Pippa. Let me own yours too."

She fisted his hair in her hands and dragged his mouth against hers.

He shifted, slipping his hand between the juncture of her thighs, feeling her most intimate spot. Her quim was wet and hot. Holding her gaze, he fisted the length of his cock and nudged it at her entrance. His length hardened, every muscle taut, aching, desperate to be within her again. Her breathing fractured and the carnal creature within her peered up at him with sensual anticipation.

Christopher pushed into her tight, wet sheath without releasing her from his gaze. Pippa's urgent gasp blended with his groan as he sank to the hilt. He withdrew and snapped his hips deep and hard. She gave a little scream, a cry of pure pleasure, her muscles tightening even further over his cock.

His balls tightened at the incredible pleasure.

"Touch me. I love it when you touch me." For when she did, it was as if she treasured each moment and would not let him go.

"Hold me, Pippa," he murmured at her ear, nipping it gently. "This ride is going to be rough."

She looped her hands around his neck and held on. And he made love with her, rough and also gentle, peppering her with praises. His Pippa responded wantonly to every touch, and illicit praises of the things he would eventually do with her—erotic spanking of her lush buttocks, nipples, and quim, mounting her from behind and fucking her deep and long, tying her to his bed with his cravat as he enslaved them to pleasure. Christopher did not hold back. Sharing his dark lustful heart with the woman he loved. And Pippa responded with burning flames of sensuality, screaming her release, dragging his seed from him long before he was ready.

Trembling from the shocking aftermath of such delirious pleasure, he twisted, so she tumbled atop him. Without a doubt, that had been the most spectacular climax of his life. She rested against his chest, panting heavily, desperately trying to catch her breath. He dragged her up until she was lying in the crook of his arm and lowered his mouth to hers, tasting her deeply, and thoroughly.

When they broke apart, she giggled, and the pure

joy in the sound pulled a smile to his lips. She curled into him to get comfortable, and a few moments later gentle snoring sounded. He held her to him, tighter than necessary. Christopher must remember to inform her she snored. He grinned, thinking how adorable her outrage would be, and then he too succumbed to the pull of sleep.

A couple of hours later, Christopher stretched, sliding his hand across the cushions and pillows searching for his Pippa. He snapped his eyes open when he did not encounter her curvy body. Scanning the semi-dark library, for the sun was valiantly peeking through the heavy drapes, he accepted that she had somehow slipped away while he slept.

Impressive. For their activities for the night had damn near killed him. They ate, they laughed, they even had some meaningful conversation other times silly and filled with laughter. But then they had made love three times, and he'd reminded himself of her innocence several times to slow the pangs of hunger which had claimed his soul. He had been insatiable with her, and she had matched his passion. Never had he thought he would be this happy at the thought of marriage and starting a family. But he could see a future with Pippa, one bright and beautiful, filled with laughter, loving, and children. A rueful smile curved his lips before it spread into a full grin. She had said yes. Pippa Cavanaugh would be his duchess.

He pushed from the mound of cushions he had made into their bed some time through the night and tugged on his trousers. A quick glance at the clock perched on the mantle revealed it to be eight in the morning. The household would already be awake. How Pippa had snuck away without waking him, he had no damn idea.

A knock sounded on the door, and the handle was tested. Christopher walked over and turned the key, so the door could be open. His butler, Jenkins, entered, a look of comical dismay entering his eyes at the disarray before he masked his reaction like a properly trained butler should.

"Beg pardon, Your Grace. Your mother and sisters are here," Jenkins said with grave dignity.

Christopher frowned. While he was close with his sisters and mother, it was not their way to descend upon him without advance notice. To do otherwise would be too improper.

"A pot of tea and toast, Jenkins. Inform them I will see them in the drawing room in about thirty minutes. Also, have one of the maids tend to the library immediately."

The butler bowed and withdrew.

Christopher wasted no time heading to his chamber and calling for a quick bath. When he entered the drawing room, he was impeccably dressed in a tan-colored riding breeches with knee-high boots, a matching tan jacket, a navy blue waistcoat, and an expertly tied cravat. He'd already predicted an invigorating ride was what he'd need in Hyde Park after facing his meddlesome family.

He paused at the somber atmosphere in the drawing room. His mother had evidently been crying, and Dear God, even his unflappable Selina appeared out of sorts. Amelia was seated on the sofa by the window tapping her foot quite anxiously. Even more telling, the pot of tea and morning edibles remained untouched.

"What has happened?" he asked, silently vowing to crush whoever had dared.

His mother gently set a newssheet atop the walnut table in the center of the drawing room.

"There is a dreadful scandal about town," Amelia said tearily.

"At eight in the morning?"

She shot him a wrathful look. "It does not matter if you are Carlyle! No one respectable will have us in their drawing rooms after this!"

Swallowing his sigh, he walked over to the table and took up the newssheet, snapping it open.

The Duke of C is a jaded libertine, and not all society believes him to be. A rake of the first order, a man scandalous in his musings and deeds hides amongst society, a dangerous wolf...a jackal in sheep's clothing. This author has it on the first most authority he is not to be trusted, he is a man with little honor and no regard for the innocent and shamelessly seduced a fine, wonderful girl at a particular garden party a few weeks ago and then refused to marry her.

He is a wicked, unprincipled libertine...a dangerous

wretch. All young ladies of virtue should steer clear! And one any mother of delicate and refined sensibilities would protect their daughter from! Not a duke of saints, I fear. But one of wicked proclivities and a man that must not be trusted.

Sincerely,
Lady W

Christopher read the article...if it could be called such, three times before he slowly lowered the paper. Pippa had submitted this to her editor, and the foolish man printed it. In Christopher's heart there was a heavy press, and not just because of the terrible scrutiny this piece of scurrilous gossip would bring to his reputation, though that was decidedly unpleasant.

A man that must not be trusted.

How could he marry a woman who believed these things of him? Who had written these things about him? He could feel the passionate disdain in each word, and they struck forcibly at his heart like bullets. Had he foolishly trusted the wrong woman? Had it all been a ploy?

He tried to recall the wild, loving moments of several hours before, but the soft, sweet lust could not be remembered, only the cold mistrust with which she had still stared at him. The intensity at which he had fallen in love with her—quick, passionate, and all-consuming— dictated that the pain rending through him was just as fierce and encompassing.

"Oh, Christopher," Selina murmured.

She had always been the sibling to understand his emotional moods best. And from the worry and pain in her voice, she sensed the turmoil churning beneath the calm façade he presented.

"Christopher," his mother said with a notable quiver in her tone. "Who is this innocent person this preposterous lady claimed you seduced and abandoned? That is a serious accusation against your character and reputation."

A thought seemed to occur to her; she added, "This Lady W would not have dared print something so inflammatory and libelous unless...unless there was some truth to it?"

He flinched, a different kind of pain worming through him. Of course, that is what society would perceive. It must be true. It was printed in a damn scandal rag, but it would be true, for who would dare print such falsehood. Who would dare scandalize the duke of C falsely? His honor had been attacked, but for his mother to question it?

He dropped the newssheet uncaring it fell to the ground. "If you will excuse me, I have a meeting to attend."

His mother's gasp of shock did not move him, nor would he defend himself against these lies, not to his family. That thought was unbearable. He spun and walked away.

"I know it is not true," Selina said softly, arresting his movements. "Forgive mamma, she spoke from a place of pain and worry. We know of your honor and your true character, and we stand by you."

He nodded and continued. Miss Pippa Cavanaugh had to be confronted. What he would say he hardly knew. What he would do he could not imagine. But he needed to peer into her eyes and ask if these were her words.

If yes...then he would have nothing to say, for then he would never have possessed even a small bit of her heart and affections.

CHAPTER 15

"The Duke of Carlyle," Thompson announced, his weather-beaten faced creased in a smile. It seemed the entire household was aware of her expectations.

Pippa smoothed her peach muslin dress down her waist, despite there were no wrinkles. He had shown. She hadn't really believed it, and she felt such awful regret she had doubted him. The duke was about to make an offer for her.

Good heavens, this is happening! She lowered dazedly into the sofa a laugh rippling from her. Her, Pippa Cavanaugh, a duchess to a man she had fallen in love with. How remarkable, when only a few months ago no one in society had thought her acceptable.

"Would you like me to see him first, my dear?" her mother asked with a smile, her eyes sparkling her happiness.

Pippa had reached home this morning, only a few

minutes before her mother, and right before the breaking dawn. Everyone had just gotten a few hours' sleep before they had risen to break their fast. While they had eaten, she had told her mother of the duke's intention. How mamma had stuttered when Pippa had informed her of the duke's promise to pay a visit. Her mother had announced Pippa's expectation to the countess, and Lady Leighton had seemed quite shocked by the news. Miranda had not been down to breakfast, and Pippa was glad, for she would like to speak to her privately before any sort of public announcement was made.

"Pippa dearest, you are woolgathering."

"I would speak with him alone, mamma, just a few words. You can leave the door open," she said, vexed that a blush was rising to her face. For with every delightfully wicked thing he had done to her a few hours ago, leaving a door open seemed beyond silly.

She needed to reassure herself this was still all real. Her mother understood for she said, "I will check on tea."

Then she departed. A minute later the duke was escorted inside. Pippa stood and smiled. He was dashingly handsome and quite commanding in his bearing. There was an air of indifference around him. His lips were flat and unsmiling, and no warmth showed in his eyes. "Christopher...?"

Every instinct she possessed warned her that something was wrong—or about to go terribly wrong. A heavy feeling settled against her heart. "Is...is everything well?" Did he regret his hasty words last night? Had his family objected as she anticipated?

The eyes that peered at her were chillingly distant. "Miss Cavanaugh, have you seen this?" he asked with icy civility.

She stared at him helplessly. Miss Cavanaugh? The lover who had taken her last night with such burning passion no longer existed. This man was a stranger. And Pippa was inordinately glad her mother was not present to witness her humiliation. "What is it?" she asked, clearing the hoarseness from her throat.

"Is this truly the manner of man you believe me to be?" he asked gently, placing the newssheet onto the small table before her. "A creature who's given over to every form of vice?"

"What? Of course not. Why would you think such a thing?"

"Then enlighten me as to what this is, please."

She took the paper and stared at it in blank shock. The angry words she had written a few weeks ago. A sick dread curled through her. "I do not understand...how is this possible?" And with a dreadful flash of insight, she knew Miranda had something to do with it.

"Did you write this?" he asked softly.

"I...I did not submit this to Mr. Bell. I swear it on my honor."

The duke's mien was cold, aloof, indifferent and it

pierced her heart. She hurried over to him. "Christopher, if you'll allow me to—"

"I warned you what would happen should you slander my name," he slung with raw fury. His tone was so cutting she flinched.

"You have called my honor into question. You have brought down scrutiny on my family though I warned you of the consequences. You wantonly published filthy lies, besmirching my character, and you did not have the nerve or courage to do it as yourself, but hide behind a pseudonym while you willfully ruined another!"

"I did not post this!" she said, a desperate pain worming through her heart. Pain and doubt gripped her by the throat at the chilling indifference in his eyes and tone. "I would never have posted this, you must believe me."

He took a few steps closer, and it was then she saw that pain also glowed in his eyes. Her words had hurt him. She had offended his pride and his honor. And in doing so, she might have lost the respect and love that had been brewing in his heart for her.

***

THE HEAVINESS against Christopher's heart was an unbearable weight. Her lovely eyes glowed with pain and guilt. "You do think this of me. Every word." He hadn't thought the pain in his heart could grow. He had been hoping someone else had written it, that she had passed the mantle of Lady W to another.

"No! Of course not." She closed her eyes before opening them. "I was not the person who published it," she admitted hoarsely.

He narrowed in on the distinction. "But you wrote it?" *Please say no*.

She flinched. "Yes, but *before* I knew you, before I knew the kind, wonderful man you are, before when I thought you had callously seduced Miranda and abandoned her. I had been hurt and angry on her behalf, hurt and angry at all the cads in the world. And that hurt went into my words."

"So you wrote all those vile things about me weeks ago?"

"Yes!"

Instead of feeling lighter, his heart became even more burdensome. "But as you came to know me... your opinion changed?"

Her eyes were wide with pain and anxiety. "Yes."

He stepped closer to her, refusing to unbend at the tears pooling in her eyes. To know she had vilified him in such a manner gutted him and had wounded him in a way he hadn't thought possible. How foolish he had been in the powers he granted her over his emotions. "Then why did you still have the letter?"

A delicate hand covered her lips, and she stared at him without answering. "Would you like me to inform you, Miss Cavanaugh?"

She shook her head wordlessly, but he swore he saw the truth of it reflected in her injured eyes.

"You did not trust in the manner of man that I am. You kept that letter because you believed one day, I would show my true character as the other men in your life who had hurt and disappointed you. Despite our connection and our experiences, you did not trust me and judged me unworthy of your respect and love despite everything. That is why you kept the letter still, Miss Cavanaugh, I dare you to deny it."

"I...I...love you...I fell in love with you," she breathed roughly. "I forgot about the letter."

He stilled. "Do you trust that I would care and treasure that love. That I would never betray you with another, and that at all time your worries and cares will always be precious to me, Pippa?"

※

Do you trust me?

An odd, painful feeling was continuing to grow in Pippa's heart. "That level of trust will eventually come," she said, clasping her trembling hands before her. Evasiveness seemed the most logical defense to a question that made her heart tremble with a panic she did not understand.

He flinched, and a flare of pain brightened the silver in his eyes before his expression shuttered. "Ah...so in your mind and heart I am simply a man like any other. Like your father and that bounder Nigel Williamsfield."

I do not want to lose you, her heart cried out. "I...I...what does that have to do with the letter? I did not post it, and I suspect who did, and I am so terribly sorry. I will do all in my powers to make amends."

The duke bowed. "Good day to you, Miss Cavanaugh."

Confusion and pain rushed through her. Was he saying goodbye? "Christopher..." Pippa took a shallow breath, refusing to give in to frustrated tears. "You do not trust me either," she said hoarsely. "You believe the worst of me when I simply forgot...*forgot* I had written that dreadful letter. I did not keep it as insurance, but that is what you believe of me, yet you profess to love and want to marry me."

A piercing pain clutched her heart in a fierce grip, and then her heart shattered into a thousand pieces when he turned and walked away without another word. Pippa stood frozen, watching him go, sensing their understanding was at an end. "I'll not chase you," she whispered fiercely, recalling her mamma abandoning her pride to run after her husband. "I'll not chase you!"

It was not the first time her expectations and hopes had been dashed. *I will be quite fine*. Yet never had the vow felt so hollow and empty. Because what she felt with the duke, she had never experienced with another and refused to believe such intensity of emotions happened more than once in a lifetime.

Last night she had hoped. And she had believed. This morning...now...everything felt dark and lonely. The pain was so great it was numbing.

Her mother appeared in the doorway of the drawing room. "Is everything well, my dear?" her mother asked with a worried frown. "I...the duke is leaving?"

Pippa was afraid of speaking, afraid her voice would break. She pressed two fingers to her lips, shook her head wordlessly, and hurried from the drawing room.

In the hallway, she spied Miranda. Pippa slowed her pace. "Why did you do it?" she asked.

"I regretted it as soon as I did," she said, genuine regret in her tone. "We argued, and I was angry. I knew you were Lady W...I saw a few of the articles in your desk drawer. I saw that one tucked away and when we argued I hated that the duke could drive a wedge between us. I selfishly admit I wanted...I wanted to cause you and the duke pain. He'd singled you out, and all society whispered of was a possible match between you two. I am so sorry Pippa! For a moment, I hated you, and I hated him for wanting you over me."

The bonds of their friendship broke, and Pippa doubted it would ever be pieced back together. Unable to speak over the emotions tearing at her, she rushed pass Miranda up the stairs. She grabbed onto Pippa.

"Please forgive me," she gasped, tears spilling on

her cheeks. "I was so stupid and rash. I did not love the duke...I simply wanted to be a duchess. And because of that desire, I have behaved wretchedly to you and the duke, and I am so very sorry."

Pippa breathed raggedly. "One day I shall forgive you for the weakness displayed in your character, but it will not be today." Then she withdrew her arm from Miranda and hurried to her chamber. Over the years she'd had to rely on her resilience, she mastered herself and her emotions until she reached upstairs to her room. But once there she crumbled, sinking against the door, sliding down until she sat on the ground with her back to the door and cried.

CHAPTER 16

Three days after the dreadful confrontation with Christopher, Pippa released her breath as Mr. Bell finished reading her latest article.

His portly face was scrunched into a frown. "Let us be clear, you wish me to run this in tomorrow's paper?"

She lifted her chin. "Yes." After spending one day in bed, crying as if her heart would not be mended, she had arrived at an irrevocable truth. She had done Christopher a disservice with her words, even if she had believed Miranda at the time. They had been thoughtless and uncaring of his honor and reputation, and he deserved a public apology.

She'd also realized he wouldn't walk away from her. Not this man who'd wanted to speak to her mother because of a kiss. His honor...and the love he had for her would not see him abandon her. He was not her father, nor was he a cad like Nigel

Williamsfield. And that, she wanted to say to his face. Before she slapped him and then kissed him. The tearing hurt of the last few days could have been avoided, but perhaps it had been necessary. For now, they would learn how to navigate their relationship better. "Yes, I am certain I wish it to be published," she said.

Miss Tilby and Mr. Bell shared a speaking glance.

"Lady W...Miss Beaver...all of London will be out to view this...this..."

She smiled grimly. "Spectacle?"

Miss Tilby stepped closer to her. "Yes. Your identity as Lady W will be made public."

Pippa nodded. "I'm quite aware what I am sacrificing, Mr. Bell. Will you run it?"

Glee lit in his eyes. "With all pleasure."

Pippa turned and walked away, a lump forming in her throat. Christopher might see the article and just toss it in the fire, but she dearly hoped he would forgive her. She hoped in showing him that she was willing to step from behind the anonymity of Lady W, that she too was willing to sacrifice and that she was not a coward. He'd accused her of hating scandal and gossip but had happily aired his laundry for the public consumption. Guilt ravaged her though she had not been the one to make the decision to publish the dreadful post. And pain destroyed her heart that this chasm still lingered between them.

CHRISTOPHER HAD DEPARTED London five days ago for his estate in Derbyshire. He poured himself a glass of brandy and settled into the large, comfortable wingback chair, and for the hundredth time wondered what the hell was he doing there. He'd left London as if dogs had chased him, traveled for two days, not sleeping or eating, wanting air to breathe and to think. His townhouse was perfumed with Pippa's scent, and the memories of their time there had already started eating through his soul, so he'd fled.

I simply forgot. You do not trust me either.

Softly spoken refrains which had been haunting him.

Could the explanation indeed be that simple? And was he too undeserving of her trust to so readily believe the worst of her? He heaved a frustrated sigh and raked a hand through his hair. Everything had been too chaotic, and he had not been able to speak with her mother. Their marriage would start on a rocky foundation, and if he wanted the forever type of love he dreamed with her, they would have to work on trusting each other more.

It still gutted him when he recalled she had not answered him. Did she honestly believe he was as unprincipled as her father and that bastard Nigel? How could they even go ahead with a marriage with such uncertainty between them? Questions he wondered at every day and night, haunting the halls of the mansion like a damn specter because he had been unable to sleep.

Christopher pushed to his feet and strolled to the windows overlooking the vast lawns of his estate. They would have to find a way to press forward. He had taken her virtue, debauched her thoroughly several times, forgetting to protect her against pregnancy. And had walked away from her despite the pain and confusion he'd seen in her eyes.

It left a bitter flavor in his mouth, and he couldn't help thinking he had let her down as well, broken the tentative trust she'd placed in him by walking away. He would marry her, and nothing could dissuade him from that promise. He hoped they would be able to mend the hurt of their thoughtless words and actions, and not allow it to fester in their heart and marriage. The last thing he wanted was a cold union devoid of mutual trust and respect like many he witnessed within the *haut monde*.

He had been a damn fool in racing from London as if he fled from demons.

A knock sounded, and he glanced around as Selina sailed inside, a forced bright smile on her face.

"Darling, this is where you had run off to! Licking your wounds in private? How droll?" her eyes laughed at him, but he could see the concern.

"I've been here only a few days, Selina. What in God's name are you doing here?"

"To be honest, Percy and I headed this way, and well, my instincts urged me to stop here before we headed down to our estate. I daresay it is a good thing I did!"

Conveniently explained, but no doubt she suspected he would come here and decided to be her usual meddlesome self. She sat in a high wing-back chair and contemplated him. He turned his back to her, pensively staring out the window. She had intruded upon his privacy, and he was not in the mood to pretend polite chit-chat was now acceptable.

"It has always seemed to me you were forever the duke. So rigid and proper even before you walked on the wild side with that gypsy girl," she said softly. "Have I ever told you I was glad you fell in love with her?" There was a long pause then she continued, "Truly I did. Afterward, you became so very reserved and cold with your passions. I always sensed another layer to your character, but you've kept it hidden until these past weeks. I credit the shift in your reaction to Miss Cavanaugh, and I suspect you have fallen in love with her. I am not sure what happened. Did she cry off because of the article?"

"No," he said, and would not offer any more explanation for Selina would tell Amelia, who would tell their mother and after that, he could not account for how this conversation would leak.

"But you do love her?"

"Desperately," he said with frankness. *And I am a damn fool.* He shouldn't have buried his head in the sand here, working out his damn feelings by himself. Trust started with communication, and from the beginning, he should have allowed his anger to cool and returned to her immediately. Instead, he had been holed up in Derbyshire for almost a damn week.

"Good. I'm not sure if you've seen this?"

A crinkle of paper had him turning around. "Not another damn scandal sheet," he all but snarled.

"This one I think you'll want to see," she said with amusement.

He strolled over to her and took the paper.

Dear Duke of C and the public,

This author passionately declares that the Duke of C is no cad, or libertine, or an unlovable cretin. This author knows this...because I am irrevocably in love with him and know the kind, wonderful, and steadfast heart of his character. He is a man to be admired and emulated, and he has my dearest love.

Duke of C...I am sorry, and I hope you will forgive me. I wrote that letter when I thought you were a libertine. How wrong every placed word was and I am not ashamed to confess my change of heart. Since I've met you, I have known love...joy...happiness and hope for a different future. I love you, I trust you, and if your sentiments remain the same, meet me at the south-east corner of the Serpentine River in Hyde Park at noon this Sunday. I will be in a bright yellow gown and hat.

P.S.: I will not hide my declaration and apology behind a pseudonym.

Yours forever.

Miss Pippa Cavanaugh writing as Lady W.

His heart almost burst from his chest when his gaze narrowed in on the date. "This was printed two days ago," he said gruffly. Worse. "It is tomorrow she will be at Hyde Park."

Selina smiled, her eyes watchful. "I wondered after such a terribly romantic declaration if you would ignore her. Society is terribly titillated, and I daresay everyone will be coming to meet you as well. Just to observe the spectacle. Mamma is of course beside herself, but I do find it...simply wonderful."

Making it to London by tomorrow afternoon was impossible. The idea of her sitting there, waiting for him to show, and believing he had ignored her apologies and sentiment almost pulled a cry of denial from his lips.

"I must leave now," he said, dropping the paper, rushing from the room, and calling for his fastest horse.

CHAPTER 17

Pippa's nerves felt stretched to the breaking point. Would he come? She had bared herself to him...to society and the *ton* would show up at the meeting point as if they attended a play at Vauxhall. Society would confirm that Miss Pippa Cavanaugh was indeed Lady W...and they would know she was desperately in love with the Duke of Carlyle.

What did you think...say when you saw my words of love? Did you scoff, laugh?

And amid those doubts, she recalled the tender emotions that had been in his eyes the night he took her on their greatest adventure.

Pippa reached a bench in the park and sat. Several ladies stared at her, their expression ranging from shock to admiration. She did not pay them any attention. Instead she opened the final chapters of *Oliver Twist*. If she did not read and divert her mind from it all, she would expire from the anxiety coursing through her.

What if he did not come...what if he loved her no longer. She recalled his words when she'd expressed her fear of loving him. *Let it not be a fear because you own my heart, Pippa. Let me own yours too.* And she smiled, pushing aside the doubts.

Almost an hour after the time Pippa had stipulated the duke had not shown. The fashionable people walking along the paths had increased significantly, for they did not move on. But seemingly waiting as well to see if the duke showed.

Many chattered behind their hands, and a few laughed. Others seemed sorry. To Pippa, their reaction did not matter, only that Christopher had not shown. She tried to be brave, keeping her head up, and the tears suppressed.

But inside, she died slowly and painfully.

The crowd dispersed long before Pippa gave up.

She went through an agony of indecision. *Should I stay or leave?* But in the end, that tiny hope that Christopher loved her as she adored him, was enough to keep her there for another two hours. It was the slight drizzle which forced her to secure her book, stand, and make her way home, her heart and reputation so broken and torn she doubted they would ever be mended.

CHRISTOPHER MADE it to London and southeast

corner of the Serpentine River in Hyde Park five hours after the allotted time. The few benches dotting the landscape were empty, and he spied no young lady in a bright yellow gown. His senses remained dormant, and he knew Pippa was no longer there. The fact he had reached even a minute after the time would have gutted her. And it destroyed him, for he didn't want her to believe, even for a second, that he had not cared enough to come.

A few ladies and gents strolling by sent him appalled looks, for his appearance was decidedly disheveled—his top hat had been lost sometime during his mad dash, his boots were splattered with mud, and his clothes were wrinkled. He had driven his horse at a hard pace, and still, he'd missed Pippa. The rains and the mud-clogged roads had been a hindrance, but he'd pushed. Only pausing to switch horses at an Inn.

And I've missed you.

He did not tarry long, once more mounting the tired horse and trotting through the busy streets to Russell Square. Upon arriving, he saw Lady Cavanaugh hurrying down the steps with a small valise in her hands. Footmen were strapping portmanteaux to the carriage. Christopher dismounted and indicated to one of the countess's footmen to take the horse to the mews for oats, water, and a rubdown.

Lady Cavanaugh had turned at his voice, and she gasped upon recognizing him. He made his way over to her, and her eyes widened at his appearance. Regret punched through him to see that she had been crying. A quick scan inside the carriage did not reveal Pippa.

"Lady Cavanaugh," he began gruffly. "I rode through the night and the rain to make it but was not in time."

Her lower lip trembled, and she stepped closer to him. "I've never seen my darling Pippa so heartbroken. She believes..." the baroness cleared her throat. "She believes she has lost your love and her reputation."

He sent a searching glance at the townhouse. "Where is she?"

"I fear we've overstayed our welcome here, and I cannot blame the countess. It seems Pippa's revelation as Lady W is a scandal too much for them to bear."

"I will fix it," he promised. "As my duchess, everyone will clamor to be accepted by her. Not the other way around."

The baroness closed her eyes briefly. "You love her then?"

"With every emotion in my heart."

"She has left with a lady's maid to Mr. Radley's Hotel in Ranelagh Gardens in Liverpool. Tomorrow she will board a ship to see her father. I do not think she plans to return anytime soon."

His heart in his throat, he bowed, and turned around. Christopher made his way home, had a bath, and made himself presentable. Then he called for his carriage. First, he would make his way to her publisher, then he would head to Liverpool and find his love.

※

Pippa stood at Canning dock at Liverpool, awaiting instructions to board her ship to New York. Her ticket had already been checked along with Molly's, the maid the countess had allowed to accompany Pippa on her journey. Their two valises had already been collected and stacked to be carried on board by a porter, and now she waited with the other passengers in the waiting room, anticipating boarding any minute now.

Mamma had insisted she would be fine amidst the rumors exploding through society. Pippa felt like a coward running away, but everything was too painful for her to stay. She needed the time away to heal, though she doubted any measure of peace would be found in New York.

Mamma was returning to Hertfordshire Crandleforth having cashed the draft of the thousand pounds, which had been sent in the letter by Miss Calvert. Mamma hadn't allowed a puffed-up sense of pride to prevent her from using the money. In truth, she had muttered the lady owed them far more than the thousand pounds. Still, it would go a far way in helping with the burden of managing the estate.

Pippa sighed, hoping that in the two-week long journey to New York from Liverpool, this awful agony inside her heart would ease. She lowered herself onto one of the chairs, and the well-dressed lady beside her shifted, the newspaper crinkling between her fingers.

It was then Pippa caught a mention of the duke. Her heart twisting, she looked away, but then she was compelled to return her regard to the article. She frowned at some of the words her eyes detected.

Love you...

My heart...

She gasped when she saw *Pippa*.

"Pardon me," she said, leaning toward the lady. "Might I borrow your newssheet for a few minutes."

The lady smiled and handed over the sheet. Pippa gripped each end of the paper shocked to see it was an article from Mr. Bell's publication.

Dear Miss Pippa Cavanaugh.

I got your invitation to meet you along the Serpentine. I confess I was in Derbyshire when I got the news, and I traveled immediately to town, but I missed you, a thing I regret most keenly, for I wanted nothing more in this world than to see you there. For you see, I must declare to you and the world, I love you with every part of me, and with every emotion in my heart. You are a lady unlike any I've ever had the privilege to know. You are fearless with your desires, bold and witty in your thinking, kind and loyal, and I know it is me you love,

Christopher Worth. Be my duchess, my wife, and my friend, Miss Cavanaugh. I urge you to complete my heart, for, without you, I am but a shadow.

Please meet me at the southeast corner of the Serpentine. Our bench awaits.
Sincerely,
Christopher Worth, the Duke of Carlyle.

Pippa read it twice before she burst into tears, shocking the other passengers. A handkerchief was quickly offered which she used to dab her cheeks. Handing over the newssheet, she scrambled to her feet and made her way from the room. Molly hurried after her, having the good sense not to ask any questions even though she did shout about the luggage once.

Just over an hour after seeing the article, Pippa along with her maid, was aboard a train, steaming its way to London. She couldn't stop crying and laughing, and she was certain everyone might think she was destined for Bedlam. A few hours later she embarked at Euston, and a hack was hailed to take her to the park.

Pippa's nerves jangled with excitement and such hope that by the time she arrived at the southeast section of the park she was a wreck. Her eyes widened to see several members of the *ton* avidly gathered. But her eyes were for the man who stood staring across the river, his back to her. Every sense within her came alive, and her heart thundered.

The applause and cheers that broke out at her arrival had Christopher spinning around. His palm pressed over his heart and the profound relief in his gaze was mirrored in hers. A sudden bout of shyness attacked her, and her steps faltered. He made his walk over to her in long strides and drew her into a fierce, scandalizing hug. He did not seem to care that the entire *haut monde* was present.

She returned his embrace, fiercely, before stepping away from him.

"How utterly ugly you look," he murmured, tenderly brushing a loose wisp of hair behind her ear.

She hiccupped a laugh. "One day I'll learn the art of pretty crying," she murmured huskily.

Powerful emotions darkened his eyes. "Please, do not. There is nothing I would change about you, Pippa. Nothing." Then he closed his eyes. "Forgive me for being an ass. I should have stayed. Ignored the pride and hurt and stayed. I will never walk away again when we have a disagreement. I want our marriage to be based on trust, honesty, and communication."

She smiled. "Mayhap I should have chased you just a little bit. You are worth everything."

"Marry me, Pippa," he said. "Be my duchess, my lover, and my friend. I love you."

It felt as if sunshine burst in her heart. "Yes."

EPILOGUE

Pippa and Christopher were married late August at St. George's Square to the delight of the *ton*. Many were able to witness the joining of what had been declared the most scandalous match of the decade. Almost everyone had remarked that only the grandest of romances would have taken the duke to the altar. And that it could have only been a woman of such strong resolutions, and a kind heart as Miss Pippa Cavanaugh who could have done it.

Pippa had delayed traveling to see her father and had sent a letter on to him instead. Miss Calvert had replied with good news, and it had made Pippa happy to know that he had recovered nicely, though she took some pleasure in not responding to the last two letters he sent begging for a visit. She did write to him and told him she forgave him, and one day perhaps she would visit New York and meet her siblings, but not at his convenience or insistence.

Before doing some traveling with her beloved husband, she would direct her attention on restoring her mother's standing in society, and the estate her father had abandoned.

They planned to visit Europe, before traveling to New York, and then onto Boston.

Her duke indulged all her desires and doted on her with a passion Pippa hadn't thought possible. And she had fallen more deeply into love with him than she'd ever imagined. She wondered if she would ever stop being incredulous and in awe over how much he loved her.

"You can turn around now," she said, laughing lightly.

The shadow of her husband loomed over her, and she lifted her lashes to peer up at him.

"My wicked, delightful, minx," he murmured.

A profound weakness invaded her limbs at the promise of pleasure in his eyes. Pippa was splayed naked atop their silken sheets, her legs spread wantonly, her breast arched, and four silken cravats beside her on the bed.

"Ravish me, my darling."

Her love came over her and pressed a kiss to her lips. She did not resist when he circled her wrists and tied them together with his silken cravat to the bedpost.

The quirk of his lips was pure, heated sensuality. "I love you, my duchess."

Another kiss, this one infinitely tender. "And I

love you," she breathed. "Take me on all your wicked adventures, my love."

And for the long, wicked night, her love did.

The End

Reviews are Gold to Authors

Gentle Readers:

THANK you for reading **Misadventures with the Duke**!

I hope you enjoyed the journey to happy ever after for Christopher and Pippa. Reviews are a very important part of reaching readers, and I do hope you will consider leaving an honest review on Amazon adding to my rainbow. It does not have to be lengthy, a simple sentence or two will do. Just know that I will appreciate your efforts sincerely.

CONTINUE READING FOR A SNEAK PEEK INTO THE
NEXT BOOK OF THE SERIES

JOIN MY NEWSLETTER

Sign up for my newsletter to be among the first to hear about my new releases, and read excerpts you won't find anywhere else. And from time to time I will do giveaways in my newsletter!

SignUp Now
www.stacyreid.com/connect

WHEN THE EARL WAS WICKED EXCERPT

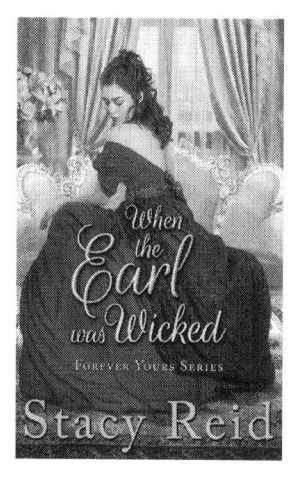

"His touch awakens her desire, and his kiss demands surrender."

Lady Verity Ayles will do whatever it takes to protect herself from a vile cur, no matter how scandalous or perilous it may be. And that means aligning with James Radcliffe, the Earl of Maschelly--a scoundrel who spends his days in sin and self-indulgence, and his nights in reckless pursuits. Clearly, a man any young lady of good sense and reputation should stay away from.

Grab a Copy Today

James had clawed his way from poverty to the fringes of the ton using his wits and fists. His wicked reputation encourages ladies to approach him for clandestine affairs, never for anything as outrageous as Lady Verity's request--to teach her how to fight. And in exchange, she will instruct him on all the refined manners a hulking, ruthless, fighting brute as himself needed to net a lady of quality. Never a man to resist a challenge or the company of a beautiful lady, James agrees, and soon finds himself falling endlessly in love with a woman who may never see him as the man of her dreams.

CHAPTER 1

London, 1840

Shortly before eight o'clock on a Wednesday evening, Lady Verity Elizabeth Ayles knocked on a particular door at 86 Eaton Square, Eaton Square Gardens. To any passing onlooker, she presented as a fashionably attired woman with an elaborate hat covering her vibrant auburn hair and a dark veil obscuring her face. A black umbrella was clutched in one of her hands, and the other hand once again lifted the lion head knocker and slammed it insistently against the large oak door.

All delicate inquiry had said the man she wanted to see would be at home tonight. Despite the preeminence of his title and family's history, he was not welcomed in most drawing rooms, ballrooms, gentlemen's clubs. Or so the rumors whispered.

The door was wrenched open, and a quite large

man filled the doorway. It took all of the fortitude she'd gained over the years to not wilt from his imposing frame. She drew a deep breath, trying to calm the wild pounding of her heart. She cleared her throat, and he peered down at her. Verity sucked in a soft breath at the piercing brilliance of his green eyes, and she was grateful the veil hid the blush heating her cheeks. He looked startled for a moment. Then he glanced up and down the street, and at the disguised carriage parked opposite his iron gate.

James Daniel Radcliffe, the Earl of Maschelly, upon first glance, did not appear either a libertine, a dastardly reprobate, or a man so handsome the devil clearly fashioned him to tempt women to sin. Verity thought he appeared quite ordinary in a dark, brooding manner, if somewhat unkempt. The man had outrageously answered the door himself, and as if to mock her consternation, he did so with bare feet, no jacket, his white shirt sleeves rolled to his elbows and a loosely tied cravat! Massive shoulders strained against his shirt, and his trousers indecently outlined thighs that were far too hard looking for a gentleman. The man was an aristocrat built like a dockworker.

Her cheeks went hot, her throat and belly too. How unpardonable he could make birds flutter in her stomach. A very unusual reaction, for she much preferred men who were fair and quick to laugh, those who were non-threatening in their demeanor. *Safe*. The very opposite of the man before her who loomed over six feet tall with the blackest scowl she'd ever seen on another's countenance. But it was this man her dearest friend, Lady Caroline Trenton, had advised was the perfect specimen to help Verity on the merry path of ruin. Though it wasn't ruination she sought, it was merely a possible consequence of her actions. But she would not be deterred, and she must be brave.

It was so absolutely reckless for her to be on this man's doorstep without a chaperone, no one must know she'd had the temerity to call upon the earl. Though dear Caroline had suggested a meeting with him, Verity was certain her friend did not mean for her to call on the man at his bachelor's residence, at night! So many wild and wicked rumors swirled about the earl. He was rumored to be dissolute, reckless, a gambler, a fighter, a great participant of sensual debauchery.

The Earl of Maschelly was wicked, they said.

He was not afraid of anyone, they rabidly whispered.

It was rumored a man of his nature spent his days in nothing but self-indulgence and sin, and his nights in recklessness at London's most dangerous haunts. He did not resist beauties, bedding a different Cyprian each night during the week, but no less than six on the weekend. That all sounded like balderdash to Verity's way of thinking, but he was still the man she needed. Though ruin and disgrace hovered. She needed him for her freedom, so she would never feel helpless or afraid ever again. He was the second step in reclaiming her dignity and her dreams.

She lowered her gloved hand which had been poised to beat the lion head knocker. "Lord Maschelly, I presume?"

Verity did not dare assume it was the butler who had opened the door in such a distinct state of dishabille. Indeed he would be fired immediately. She did not dare assume the butler would also possess the dark green eyes reflecting the forest after a night of rain, or it would be the butler in possession of such raven black hair and sensually full lips. He wasn't handsome in the soft manner or anything like the refined and elegant men of the *ton*. This was all hard edges and so compelling she stared helplessly, absurdly grateful he could not see that she gawked like a silly miss.

The man regarded her with a fascinated eye, then drew an audible breath. "And who the hell are you?" His tone was crisp and stinging as the lash of a whip.

She winced at his uncouthness, appalled at his lack of civility. But there was nothing she could do about that, not when she needed him. And strangely, his impertinence calmed her. "First, I apologize for calling without notice and in such a clandestine manner. It was unavoidable since you've ignored my previous letters asking to meet discreetly. It is of the utmost importance I have a private audience with you, my lord."

"Why?"

Verity took a steadying breath. "I have a proposition for you, one that is best discussed in privacy."

His scowl went even darker. "Well hell, no one has ever offered it up on my front step before in such an obvious manner."

She gasped at the sheer effrontery of his lewd suggestion. Verity was quite aware of what he referred to, and almost turned around and departed then at his lack of gentlemanlike manners. The words were cutting and hinted at a cynicism she'd not expected.

"I am a *lady*, my lord, you will comport yourself accordingly and what I have for you is a business proposal," she said, careful not to choke on her mortification, grateful her voice did not tremble.

Darkness and fog blanketed the area, and the few gas lamps shed little light. All that was convenient to her disguise, but she felt nervous and uncertain.

"A lady? At my home at this hour, without a chaperone?" This bit was drawled with mocking cynicism.

"Yes," she replied pertly, "I daresay a woman of my years can venture out without undue speculation and ruin." Such ridiculousness for if she was discovered, her life, and reputation would be in shambles. But Verity was desperate and afraid, and he was someone who could help her put her nightmares to rest, even if he did not know it. "And the gentlemanly conduct would be to invite me inside away from possible speculation and the dreadful chill in the air."

Those beautiful eyes stared at her veil as if he wanted to discern the features beneath the disguise. Nervous energy had her tugging at the piece of lace brushing against her chin. Then to her relief and amazement, he stepped back and bid her entrance.

Verity made her way inside, startled at the overwhelming darkness. No lamplight shone in the hallway, but she could discern enough to follow the earl to a large and tastefully furnished drawing room. A fire blazed merrily in the hearth, and the earl waved at her to sit. She lowered herself into the plush sofa, anxious that he remained standing.

"Will you also sit, my lord?"

The earl arched a brow, and it was then she noted the faint discoloring on his left cheek.

Verity became aware of the subtle scent of his sweat as he moved closer. And he walked as if hurt, a slight tilt to the left, favoring his side. The brawn of his body was overwhelming. He was tall, so much broader than she. A small part of her wanted to move away. But her courage could not falter now, not when she had reached so far. Inexplicably she felt at once both threatened and secure. Foolish to feel safe for she did not know the manner of man he was. Just what the rumors said. And she felt silly for resting her plans on the entirety of idle speculations.

"Will you need refreshment?" he demanded in that terrible uncivil way of his.

"There is no need to be boorish," she sniffed.

"I did not invite you here."

Verity flushed. "You did not, and I apologize for the intrusion. It is still not an excuse for your incivility."

"Do you wish for a drink?"

"No," she said with polite stiffness.

There was a decanter of amber liquid on the oak table before her, an empty glass, and a white handkerchief that had a suspicious red stain. She had interrupted his drinking. He poured his amber liquid into the glass, and then lowered himself into the sofa opposite her.

"What is this proposal?" he said, impatience coloring his tone.

She cleared her throat delicately, wondering where to start with her very scandalous and unorthodox request. "Society says a dance from you has the power to ruin any young lady. And perhaps that is why you've never asked anyone to the dance floor."

"And do you want ruin, do you?" his voice was a purr of sin and darkness, and some unfathomable emotion she did not understand. It had the edge of anger, causing a ripple of discomfort to course over her skin.

She took a steadying breath and met his curious gaze, ignoring his interruption. "They say you are an untested king in the underground pugilist world of London. That you made your fortune on the blood and fractured limbs of others. Those other men... lords and those common folks, admire you...revere you even. Your nose has been broken three times, your ribs cracked numerous times, yet you've never been beaten. You understand honor *and* dishonor. You are a fair man but can be dangerous when crossed. You've been the 11th Earl of Maschelly for seven years now, and the loudest rumor in the *ton* is that you are now seeking a wife, preferable an heiress, whose father has political connections to aid you in becoming the Member of Parliament for the area where your earldom is situated."

He was silent for the longest moment. Shuffling sounds crept into the still of the night, and Verity glanced around nervously. He gripped his glass, drinking deeply, his gaze never leaving her veiled expression.

"So you know something about my reputation... and you are here...alone with me. Curious. Who are you?"

She licked her lips. "I cannot own to my identity at the moment. Not until a bargain has been struck."

His stare was unnerving, intense, and quite intelligent. "What do you want?"

The words lashed at her, and she stiffened. "I...I would like you to teach me to fight, my lord."

Silence fell upon the room, and he stared at her as if he peered into her very soul. She felt exposed and vulnerable, because so much rode on his response to her simple yet unorthodox and scandalous question.

A response which he refrained from giving, he only stared, taking the measure of her. Had she made an error in approaching him? Had her hopes for freedom come to a sudden premature halt?

The End
CONTINUE READING...

ACKNOWLEDGMENTS

I thank God every day for my family, friends, and my writing. A special thank you to my husband. I love you so hard! Without your encouragement and steadfast support, *Misadventures with the Duke* would not be published today. You encourage me to dream, and you are always constant in your incredible support. You read all my drafts, offer such fantastic insight and encouragement. Thank you for designing my fabulous cover! Thank you for reminding me I am a warrior when I wanted to give up on so many things.

Thank you, Giselle Marks for being so wonderful and supportive always. You are a great critique partner and friend. Readers, thank you for giving me a chance and reading my book! I hope you enjoyed and would consider leaving a review. Thank you!

ABOUT STACY

Stacy Reid writes sensual Historical and Paranormal Romances and is the published author of over sixteen books. Her debut novella The Duke's Shotgun Wedding was a 2015 HOLT Award of Merit recipient in the Romance Novella category, and her bestselling Wedded by Scandal series is recommended as Top picks at Night Owl Reviews, Fresh Fiction Reviews, and The Romance Reviews.

Stacy lives a lot in the worlds she creates and actively speaks to her characters (aloud). She has a warrior way "Never give up on dreams!" When she's not writing, Stacy spends a copious amount of time binge-watching series like The Walking Dead, Homeland, Altered Carbon, watching Japanese Anime and playing video games with her love. She also has a weakness for ice cream and will have it as her main course.

I am always happy to hear from readers and would love to connect with you via my Website, Facebook, and Twitter. To be the first to hear about my new releases, get cover reveals, and excerpts you won't find anywhere else, sign up for my newsletter, or join me over at Historical Hellions, the fan group for my historical romance author friends, and me!

Follow me on BookBub

Printed in Great Britain
by Amazon